The Brightening

Leila Sahabi

The
Brightening

Prologue

The Decision

"Well, face it!" Hugo pointed out. "The current system is not working!" The leads of the Lucinian government were arguing about the best way to handle the… situation with the Darkened. Nearly two years ago, a growing group of people set on taking over the planet for themselves had been discovered, and the government was torn on how to handle it. Hugo, the logical possessor of Blue light magic, believed that the best option was to keep the magic a secret from the common people. How could the Darkened destroy the magic if they were not aware of its existence in the first place?

"But they are our citizens! They need to know

that their government cares about them," Clementine insisted. She, with her Orange light magic, was very social, and the idea of a harsh, mysterious, secretive government did not appeal to her in any way. In her opinion, separating citizens from the government was the way to *cause* issues, not solve them.

"None of you understand!" Edith, the lead with Red light magic, shouted. "*We* are not the problem. *They* are. Which means that the only thing that must change is them. We should fight them."

At this, quiet Helena, with her Yellow light magic, finally spoke up, "We do not want a war! We cannot sink to their level! Violence is so primitive!"

"And what do *you* suggest we do, then?" Edith snapped. She was well aware that Helena wanted neither to fight, nor to hide.

"Will you all quit arguing? We are meant to be united *against* the Darkness, and look at us now! If we continue like this, they will easily divide us and take control," said Norman, the holder of Purple light magic.

"Norman is right," Otis, the lead with Green light magic, agreed. "Why can't we all just agree that the best option is to keep the magic a secret? The less the people know, the easier it is to control them, and to stop the Darkened before they start something." Otis, though he also did not want to hide behind a stone wall for the rest of his life, had decided to base his decision on what was objectively the best for Lucina's future, instead of his own emotions.

"That is in no way what I meant!" Norman shouted. He agreed with Clementine; the citizens would become suspicious and side with the Darkened if the leads tried to keep the magic a secret.

"We have to fight," said Victor. "Yes, people will get hurt, but it is a risk we must take. It is the best way to get rid of the Darkened, once and for all." Victor possessed the rare Infrared light magic, and therefore tended to be impulsive.

"What we *have* to do is protect the people," said Otis. "And the best way to accomplish that is to keep the magic as far away from them as possible."

"But what about the citizens who possess magic and are not aware? What happens when the Darkened target them? Is that really protecting the people?" argued Leonora. She believed that the citizens should know of the power they might possess. After all, she hated to imagine how normal her life would have been if she had not discovered that she had Ultraviolet light magic. She also knew that some of the citizens had the potential to greatly benefit the Light side, if only they knew they had magic.

This argument was nothing new. For two years, now, the leads of the planet Lucina had been debating on whether they should hide from the Darkened, fight them, or do something else entirely.

When the small group of magicals had first migrated to Lucina, they had fully believed that Lucina would be the perfect, peaceful home, especially in comparison to Earth. Though the inhabitants of Lucina had come from many civilizations worldwide, they could all agree that Earth was full of power struggles and wars.

For the first few years, life on Lucina was exactly what they had expected. They had used magic to change the orbit and rotation of the planet to have a time system exactly the same as Earth's, but counting from the year they arrived. It was unnecessary, but convenient. They had organized an annual magic contest for the citizens' entertainment. They (specifically Hugo and his team of Blue magicals) had studied light magic and learned that there were eight forms, Infrared, Red, Orange, Yellow, Green, Blue, Purple, and Ultraviolet. They had also learned that people could be born with a range of different connection percentages to a certain color of light—not all high enough to perform magic. However, that was decided not by genetics (like they had originally assumed) but by fate. Through this discovery, they realized that not everyone on Lucina possessed light magic.

In fact, some citizens of Lucina were completely the opposite: the evil Darkened. And now, those citizens were destroying the perfect society that the leads had built.

Though they could not seem to agree on how to resolve the conflict, each of the leads knew that the decision would have to be made someday soon. Every day that the decision was put off, the Darkened grew in power.

That 'someday soon' suddenly became much sooner as the door to the Meeting Room slammed open. In burst Callie, a new recruit. "We have caught three more Darkened spies in our staff!" she exclaimed.

"Thank you for letting us know, Callie," said Helena.

Callie nodded and exited the room.

The leads glanced at one another anxiously. They all knew that they needed to come to a decision, or the Darkened would become too powerful.

"Let us take a vote," Otis announced. "Everyone must decide to either fight or hide."

"All in favor of keeping the magic secret, raise your hand," said Hugo, his right arm up.

Otis raised his hand.

Hesitantly, so did Clementine. "Well, I don't want the citizens to revolt, but I don't want them to die either."

Helena and Norman followed her lead, raising their hands as well.

Edith, Victor, and Leonora frowned, keeping their hands down.

"Well, it is decided, then," Otis announced. "We will keep the magic a secret."

Edith opened her mouth to argue, but Otis stopped her.

"If it does not work, fighting will be our backup plan. Are we all in agreement?" He asked.

The rest of the leads nodded reluctantly.

1

Personality Test

Thousands of years later, city of Green, Lucina…

I stared at the screen of my computer. Same, old pie chart. Same, old eight equal slices. Hey, at least I didn't know what these tests meant, yet. Had I known at the time, I would've been devastated. From the fourth grade to the seventh grade, all students in any city on the planet Lucina were required to take a survey. Twice a year, we'd fill out seemingly useless questions about our personalities, and, at the end, we'd receive a pie chart with eight slices in the colors red, orange, yellow, green, blue, purple, a kind of grayish purple and a similar grayish red, plus a list of what percent of the circle each color filled. Nobody knew what they meant—not even our teachers—however, the government, for some reason, required us all to be tested, and so we took the tests, assuming that they would, in some way, be helpful.

The government on the planet Lucina was strange. They were very secretive about their work. All we were allowed to know was that each of the seven cities was governed by a main group of six, plus additional lower-ranked officials. They placed a lot of strange rules on the citizens, one of which was, of course, the surveys.

As boring as my results always were, my Yellow side would've been happy that, A) this was the last time I'd have to take one of these tests ever again, and B) it was the last day of school.

Speaking of which, *RIIING*! And the class hurriedly shoved their belongings into their bags and exploded out of the room, crowding in the hallway along with all the other classes. Everyone was in a hurry to escape school. If there's one thing that all thirteen year olds can agree on, it's that school is awful, though everyone has their own unique reason for thinking this. For some, it's pure boredom. Others, the people around them. Others, yet, fear of failure, and so on. For me, it's loneliness.

Oh, stop it! I already know what you're thinking: 'But, Zia, you have so many friends!' I already know that. There's just one issue. I don't fit into a specific category, and, therefore, don't exactly have real friends. Sure, I get good grades, but I'm not a "nerd." I have lots of friends—lots of friend *groups*, even—but I'm not necessarily "popular." I always seem to relate to more than one character in books or movies. I can never choose which I'm most like. If I were asked to classify my personality into a personality type, I would say none of them. I'm just… me. I have so many parts to my personality that I can fill whatever role is missing in a friend group, and I assume that's why I'm a part of so many groups. These groups are all friends, sure, but none are really my *best* friends. There is a big difference. Friends are somewhat close, but *best* friends feel like family. Friends laugh at jokes occasionally, but *best* friends share inside jokes. I wanted the kind of friendship that you'd read about in a book. Friends that go on adventures together, and are always there for each other. That was what I wanted, and what I knew I wouldn't get.

As I was nearing the door to freedom, I heard a familiar voice behind me. "Zia, wait for me," called one of my friends, Adella Azure.

Adella wasn't a part of any of my groups, but we were still somewhat of friends, since we'd been in the same class in fourth grade, and we'd gotten along. She was about my height, with light brown hair a few inches past shoulder length. Her eyes were amber colored, and her face had a few freckles. She was wearing a black t-shirt over white shorts. She always seemed to dress like that—colorless. As much as I wouldn't wear what she wore every day, Adella was an overall fun person to hang out with and someone who made class a lot more entertaining in fourth grade.

"I'm waiting," I replied, pulling over to the edge of the hallway and stopping.

When she reached me, she began to speak eagerly. "What did you get on the survey?"

Everyone in my grade already knew that my score was always the same. Most people's scores would waver. I had friends whose scores from the start of the year would be unrecognizable when compared to the scores from the end. I wondered why she'd be asking me out of nowhere, instead of someone with more interesting results. I responded anyway. "The usual. You?"

"I got 94.7 percent blue!"

2

A High Score

As all people living on the planet Lucina knew, a survey score of 75 percent or higher in any color was unusually high, making Adella's score of 94.7 percent almost impossible. It was unbelievable. I'd never met anyone, other than her, of course, who had a score over 80. Now that I thought about it, she'd never told me her scores before, so I had no way of knowing if it was anywhere near her usual score, or if her score had suddenly changed. All I knew was that it was insanely high.

"94.7 percent?" I repeated, shocked.

"Yup," she said.

"Then what happened?" I was eager to find out

how her teacher handled such a high score.

"My teacher called me to his desk after class and gave me this letter. It says—well, look for yourself." She handed me the envelope. On it was written, in sloppy handwriting, "To any seventh grade student with a consistent score above 75 percent in any of the eight colors".

Consistent? I thought. *Her score has always been this high? How is that even possible?*

Knowing that the government was in charge of the surveys, I was very curious as to what would happen when someone scored so high. I pulled out the paper inside. To my surprise, the message was very brief, and written in the same messy handwriting as on the outside:

Congratulations on achieving a high score.

Government Position Available.

Present yourself for an interview.

6:00 AM on Saturday 6/1/2122 Lucina Years

(6/1/2022 Earth Years)

Central Skyscraper of Green.

313 Olive Street

The first thing I said was "At *six in the morning?*"

"I don't care," was Adella's response.

I'm not sure how or when, but at some point, I found out that Adella, like me, was very much a night person, and hated mornings. For her to agree to wake up at six in the morning on a Saturday was unheard of. Then again, it *was* a *government* job interview in the *central skyscraper*.

On the planet Lucina, there are seven cities: Red, Orange, Yellow, Green, Blue, Purple, and Allight. The cities are separated by thousands of miles of untouched land, a decision made by our ancestors for reasons lost to history, as far as I knew. At the very center of each of these cities sat a huge, stone skyscraper, built by the very first people who migrated from Earth to Lucina at around 100 B.E.Y. (Before Earth Years). These were called central skyscrapers, and no regular citizens were ever allowed inside them. Only government workers were allowed to enter, leaving the rest of the planet to theorize about what could be hidden there, and, like most of the other strange laws, we theorized. Many genuinely believed that the government was hiding high-tech time travel equipment inside, or that they ran dangerous tests on people with toxic chemicals that no one knew about. Others believed more plausible theories, such as that the government wasn't as organized and in-control as we thought, and that they hid their weaknesses behind the thick stone bricks of the skyscraper.

"If you're so scared that I'll fall asleep, why don't you come with me?" Adella challenged jokingly.

"I will, then," I said. A thing about me is that I don't turn down challenges. Big or small, serious or humorous, I would always try my best to accept challenges. Plus, I'd get to see the central skyscraper, and what kind of a loser would turn down an offer like that?

So there I stood the next morning, half asleep, at the door to the secret government building that no one was allowed inside. The cold morning air, along with the excitement of the situation kept me awake. Adella knocked on the old, wooden door for the second time, and, unlike the first time, the door creaked open.

Inside stood a girl who looked about seventeen years old. She was of average height, dressed in a black shirt with purple stripes and black ripped jeans. Her short, dark brown hair had a bright purple streak on the right side. She had tan skin and grey eyes. "You only need to knock once," she muttered. "And there was only supposed to be *one* of you."

"The letter never said I couldn't bri—"Adella started, but a man's voice from inside the building cut her off.

"*Viola*," he yelled. " I said *I* was doing the greeting!"

The girl, Viola, rolled her eyes. "Well, Cyrus, *you* were late."

"At least I'm nice," Cyrus retorted, pushing Viola

away from the door and taking her spot. He looked about the same age and height, and he had the same brown hair and grey eyes as Viola, but he had warmer, friendlier energy.

"Sorry, that was my grouch of a sister. She still hasn't outgrown the teenage rebellion phase. Luckily, she has a mature brother who keeps her reputation safe. Oh, and you're welcome to bring your friend."

I'm just allowed in like that? I thought. *I thought this place was supposed to be all secret and off-limits.*

"Cool," said Adella. "So, what kind of job is this, exactly?"

"You'll see," he responded. "Come inside." With that, he turned around and began walking towards the back of the foyer, where I could see two elevators. We followed him into the left elevator, and we were soon on the top floor. Cyrus then led us into an office with a green sign on the half open door. The sign had a strange, fluid glow to it.

Inside the office, sitting at a dark, wooden desk was a man, maybe thirty years old, with curly black hair and green eyes. He looked up and saw me. "Cyrus, at this point, why don't you invite the whole city in?" he said, annoyed.

"You're the one who said one new trainee was not enough," Cyrus responded.

One new trainee? Does that mean Adella is the only one in the whole city with a high score? Is that why we're the only ones at the door? Wow, I thought.

"I didn't mean you could bring in random people!"

"Well—"

"Escort her out," the other man demanded.

I'm already in the skyscraper. How much harm will it really do to let me stay? Of course, it would *be breaking the laws, but if I'm not caught...*

"Oh, you really don't need to do that," I smiled. "I'll just go back the way I came."

He seemed skeptical. "You really remember?"

"Yeah!"

He glanced at the clock on the wall, thought for a moment, then said, "Fine, but only because we're short on time."

"Thank you, sir," I said respectfully, while my mind shouted, *YES!*

As I was walking down the hall looking for the perfect spot to hide, I heard the speakers on the ceiling crackle on. I quickly turned left, into another, much shorter hallway, which led to a glass door. The door opened onto a balcony. Just above the doorframe, the words, "East Balcony," were printed in big, black letters.

"All leads to the Meeting Room, please," came the green-eyed man's voice over the speakers.

Looking out into the bigger hallway, I saw Cyrus and the other man leading Adella to a room with a big, wooden door. I stepped back into the hallway the minute they closed the door behind them, and started tiptoeing toward the door. My plan was working!

Suddenly, I became aware of a sound. Footsteps. Very faint, but definitely there. I froze, holding my breath, and tried to figure out where the sound was coming from.

I wonder if I can get back to the smaller hallway fast enough. Looking back, I realized that I definitely couldn't. Just then, an old lady with a cane hobbled out of one of the offices. She had curly gray hair, dark skin, and was wearing a yellow dress. I continued holding my breath until she finally entered the room, at which point I had already started considering swim lessons to strengthen my lungs.

Tiptoeing closer, I realized that she'd left the door ajar. *Perfect!*

3

Job Interview

Peeking through the door, I saw that a large desk with eight chairs occupied the center of the meeting room. The chairs, I noticed, had cushions in the colors red, orange, yellow, green, blue, purple, and the same grayish red and purple that I'd seen in the pie chart on the survey. Were the survey and these chairs somehow connected?

Six of the chairs were occupied—the red one by an orange haired woman who looked about thirty years old, wearing a red shirt and white pants, the blue one by a younger woman, maybe in her early twenties, wearing a blue dress, the yellow one by the old woman in the hallway, the orange and green by

Cyrus and the other man respectively, and the purple one by Viola, the unfriendly girl who'd opened the door for us. The grayish red and purple seats, for some reason, were left empty.

"Hi!" said the woman in red. "My name is Rose, and your name must be Adella. Please take a seat right there." She indicated a chair on the opposite side of the desk from the colorful chairs. Adella moved to the chair. The interview was a lot more boring than I had expected, and, for most of it, I wasn't really listening. For the first half hour, I thought about various subjects, including why the last two chairs could've been left empty. Maybe they were extras? Or maybe they were old and broken? But that didn't make sense because if the chairs were connected to the pie chart in some way, the last two colors were supposed to be there. So maybe the people who were supposed to sit there had called in sick? My thoughts were interrupted when a word said by the interviewers caught my attention: *magic*.

"Your score on the survey means that you possess

very strong Blue magic," the woman in the blue seat was saying. She glanced at Adella's entirely blue outfit, which differed significantly from her usual black and white attire.

I guess she wanted to make a not-so-boring impression on the interviewers, I thought.

"Magic?" I asked, throwing the door open. I'd completely forgotten that I was not supposed to be here, let alone interrupt whatever was going on.

"You? I thought you'd left," shouted the man in the green chair.

"I—"

"Get. Out. Now."

"Please, can I know about the magic?" I begged.

"Well, she's heard about it now. We may be better off just testing her. After all, Emery, you did say that we need more recruits," said the lady in the yellow dress.

"Even if you leave today without a job, everything you've overheard must be kept secret, and you will be closely monitored from this moment on.

Spilling government secrets doesn't end well. Understand?" Emery warned me, realizing that the lady was right.

"Deal. Now can I know about the magic?"

"Yeah," said Cyrus. "What do you think all those surveys were about? We were testing your powers to see if you were qualified to join."

"What makes someone qualified?" I asked, hopeful to maybe get a chance of learning magic.

"A consistent score of 75 percent or higher in any color and you're invited to the interview. If you accept the job, you're in. If not, you continue your life as normal, on the condition that you never tell anyone about the magic."

"Oh." 12.5 percent was nothing compared to 75.

Cyrus turned back to Adella. "I'm not sure you need it to channel, since you're so powerful already, but try using this to call a ray of Blue light." He placed a clear, perfectly cut, rectangular prism of crystal on the desk.

Adella suddenly looked uncomfortable and anxious. "Uh, I don't think I can."

"Of course you can. You're one of the most powerful people ever to exist," said the woman in the blue chair.

"I really think I need more training first. Sure, I'm powerful, but I'm a beginner. I have no control over my magic."

"Let her be. She's new," said the older woman, the one in the yellow chair, smiling.

"Wait," I butted in. "Can I try?" Though I knew I didn't qualify, I was an avid reader who loved fantasy stories in which someone learned how powerful he or she was, and actually made a change in the world. Now that I could be that character in real life, I was determined to work for the government.

"If your test score was less than 75 percent in one color, you aren't connected enough to a specific light wave to do anything," explained the man in the green chair. "Plus, if it *was* higher than 75 percent, you would've been invited to the interview yourself and wouldn't have had to come along with your friend."

"Please," I tried, desperate. I was sure that, if I believed in myself, I would be able to do something with the prism. That was how it worked in the stories.

Before the man could respond, the woman in the yellow chair said, "Go ahead, dear. It can't hurt to try."

Excited, I walked up to the desk and picked up the prism.

What do I do to make it glow?

I squeezed it in my hand, I rubbed it, I stared at it, and it did... nothing. I knew it. I didn't qualify. I couldn't do anything. I would never have the chance to be a legendary hero. It was a mere vain dream of a desperate child.

4

Persistence and Failure

Still, I wasn't the type of person to give up so fast. When things went wrong for the characters in the books I read, they didn't give up and go stand in a corner. They kept trying until they succeeded. So I decided to try again.

"Can you maybe… train me or something?" I asked.

"I don't know, but we can try," Rose smiled. She turned to the rest of the group and said, "It'll be a challenge, guys. It'll be fun! And imagine if we CAN actually train someone. Imagine the benefits."

"Well, firstly," said the man in the green chair, still seemingly unconvinced. "What was your survey score?"

"12.5 percent on everything," I announced, hope rising in me.

Simultaneously, the six members of the group in front of me developed the most shocked expressions I had ever seen.

"That's…" began the woman in the blue chair.

"Lower than the lowest possible score," finished Viola. "That makes all the colors equal. That's impossible."

"Let us handle this privately, girls," said the older woman, handing Adella a piece of paper and gesturing towards the door. "Read this while you wait. It'll explain everything you need to know about magic."

As we shut the heavy door behind us, both of our professional faces dissolved, and we started to speak at the same time.

"Did you know?" I asked.

"Can you believe it?"

So, she didn't know then. "The government's hiding magic," I whispered, mainly trying to assure myself that I hadn't imagined it all. I felt too conscious for this to be a dream, but it was surreal. MAGIC? "It's the one thing the conspiracy theorists missed."

"I guess they were onto something, though," she pointed out. "I never would've thought that the government was hiding magic."

"Yeah," I agreed. "So that paper is going to explain it all?"

"I guess."

We sat down on the cold stone floor—the same, strange, material as the walls were made of—with our backs to the door, and read the paper.

LIGHT MAGIC

LIGHT MAGIC IS A POWERFUL ENERGY BENDING TECHNIQUE THAT CAN BE USED BY SPECIAL PEOPLE WITH STRONG CONNECTIONS TO A COLOR OF LIGHT. EVERY HUMAN BEING IN THE UNIVERSE HAS A COLOR THAT HE OR SHE IS CONNECTED TO MORE THAN OTHER COLORS, AND THIS CAN SHOW UP IN THEIR PERSONALITIES, CHOICE OF CLOTHING, AND SOMETIMES EVEN

LOOKS. THE SIX COMMON COLORS ARE RED, ORANGE, YELLOW, GREEN, BLUE, AND PURPLE, ALTHOUGH THERE IS A VERY SLIM CHANCE THAT ONE WILL BE CONNECTED TO ULTRAVIOLET OR INFRARED LIGHT. HOWEVER, ONLY THOSE WITH LIGHT CONNECTIONS ABOVE 75 PERCENT ARE ABLE TO IMPLEMENT SOLID USE OF THEIR MAGIC. IF ONE'S CONNECTION PERCENTAGE FALLS BELOW THE MINIMUM, THEIR MAGIC IS UNSTABLE AND DIFFICULT TO CONTROL, MAKING IT DANGEROUS TO USE. DURING ANCIENT TIMES, LEADERS ON EARTH DISCOVERED SMALL GROUPS OF MAGICAL INDIVIDUALS SPREAD ALL OVER THE PLANET. COLLECTIVELY, THEY DECIDED TO SEND THE KNOWN MAGICAL INDIVIDUALS TO A DISTANT PLANET THAT THEY NAMED LUCINA TO ASSURE THAT NON-MAGICAL HUMANS WOULD NOT ABUSE THE LIGHT MAGICALS. LIGHT MAGIC IS NOT GENETIC, AND ANY PERSON CAN BE BORN WITH IT, SO, IN THE MODERN DAY, THE GOVERNMENT KEEPS THE POWER A SECRET, EVEN FROM CITIZENS ON LUCINA.

The back of the paper listed all the known spells, which I skimmed through quickly. Once I reached the end, I looked up, realizing something. "The only spells are attack and defense spells," I pointed out. "What use are those? It's not like there are wars here." The seven cities were so far apart that no conflict ever arose between them.

"Yeah," Adella agreed. "I thought magic was supposed to do interesting things like make me fly."

"Oh, well. It's still magic."

I also realized that the spells only required one person to perform, and the person could be of any light connection. *So, what's the point of having multiple colors? They can't just be there for no reason. Is there something they're hiding, or am I just overthinking this?*

Suddenly, a shout came from inside the meeting room, muffled through the door, but still loud enough to hear. It was the voice of the man in the green chair. "Stop it! She is and we all know it!"

"Emery, look at the facts," reasoned the voice of the woman in blue. "She doesn't fit the description. She really doesn't act like she lost her connection.

Plus her results aren't what they'd be if she was one of them."

"She could be faking it all," Emery yelled.

"Children, arguing isn't going to do anything to solve the problem," said the older lady in the yellow chair, desperately.

"She's outside, you absolute idiots. She can hear you. Why don't you listen to Grandma Mari and shut up?" That was clearly Viola.

"You're the one yelling," Cyrus retorted.

"So are you," she shouted back at her brother.

"You people have to listen to me!" Rose insisted. "Give her a chance."

"Absolutely *not*," yelled Emery and Cyrus simultaneously, then everyone started shouting over each other.

5

Persistence Again

As curious as I was, I realized that it would be more than a little impolite to ask what (or who) the leads were arguing about, and impolite was the last trait I wanted them to associate me with. I wanted to leave a good impression in hopes that maybe it would lead to me getting hired, even without meeting the required minimum.

I tried asking again to be hired, insisting that I was sure there was some little way in which I could help, like sorting papers, or organizing desks, but I was, of course, denied and escorted outside. Meanwhile, Adella was inside, signing the paperwork. *So unfair!*

To be honest, I was more dejected than angry at the fact that Adella was hired and I was not. Unlike me, she didn't seem too excited about trying out her powers. If I were her, I'd be having the time of my life. Sadly, I was not her.

I didn't understand why she'd been given magic and I hadn't. I wanted a story too. I wanted to make a change. I wanted to help. I wanted to be a part of a *secret magic force* run by *the government*.

Give it up, I thought, leaning against the stone wall—still cold from the night. *If I were made to be a hero, the adults would know. I know nothing about magic. I'm sure everyone's life will be better if I don't join, and live a normal life. A normal, boring life.*

Absolutely not, interjected the Red in me. *Who ever got anywhere by giving up and accepting what they were told? I have to keep trying.*

So I work hard and get… connected, thought my Green.

But how? I don't think it would work, reasoned my Blue side. Suddenly, an idea sprung into my mind. An idea that might take ages to work, but would be easy enough, and, unlike trying to become magical, actually had a chance of working. The next thing I knew, I was pounding on the door, more determined than ever.

The door opened, and the woman previously seated in the blue chair, who I had later learned was named Sapphire, took one look at me, then turned and nodded behind her. She turned back to me. "Listen, the rules say no."

"But—" The door closed, cutting me off, but I wasn't done. I wouldn't be done until I was hired.

Every morning for the next two weeks, I knocked on the door of the stone skyscraper, and every morning, I was denied the job, but I kept coming back. A part of me knew that I would never actually be hired. I missed the minimum by far too much. That part, however, was never loud enough to stop me. I was too determined.

This determination was still inside of me on the fifteenth day, as I woke up and changed into my clothes.

I have a good feeling about today, I told myself, as I did every morning.

"Bye, Mom! Bye, Dad!" I called, opening the front door.

"Zia, where to?" asked my dad, who very obviously knew exactly where I was headed.

"The skyscraper," I said, hesitantly.

"What makes you want that job so badly? I just want to know why you suddenly care so much about the government."

"The interview really caught my attention, that's all," I lied. I knew very well that if the government caught me spilling their secrets, being declined the job would be the least of my worries.

"Well, if it's this important to you, all I can say is good luck… again."

"Thanks, Dad. I love you," I beamed.

Stepping out of the front door, the wind breathed ice cold air into my face, and I realized that it was abnormally cold for the middle of summer. I brushed it off, ran back inside, and quickly pulled on my favorite pink sweater, too focused on getting to the skyscraper to really care.

Hearing my knock again, the exasperated leads decided to finally let me in and actually give me an interview. *One step closer! I knew today was going to be a great day!* I thought.

I took the elevator up, then walked down to the end of the hallway, into the meeting room, where a stack of papers piled on the desk caught my eye. They were the documents to be signed to make my employment official. As Emery walked in, a plan began to brew in my mind.

"Kid, you can have the interview, but we both know that you—" he started, but I interrupted him.

Pointing out the window at a strange grid of spherical clouds, I said, "Hey, check out those clouds." They were darker than any clouds I had ever seen before.

While Emery was distracted, I snatched the paper on the top of the pile, signed it, put it on the table, and began pushing it towards him. I stopped when he muttered, "Oh, no." He saw the paper and sighed. "Fine. Just don't get in the way, and don't leave this building until I tell you that you can. This is a serious issue." He picked up a pen and hastily signed the document.

"Yes, sir," I smiled. "Wait, but what's a serious issue? Those clouds? What are they anyway?"

"Those, child, are sphormites, and they're the worst ones I've seen in my entire life," he said, eyes still locked on the ominous, gray spheres in the sky.

6

Chaotic First Day

"But what's a sphormite?" I asked, quickly standing and following Emery as he rushed out the door.

He ignored me and continued walking through the hallway. We ran into Viola, and Emery hurriedly informed her of the situation before sending me off with her. She led me to the foyer, where I assumed she'd tell me to leave, then to the corner, where she put her hand on the floor, pressed lightly, and stepped back as the stones forming the floor in that area rose slightly. She picked up the rectangle of floor to reveal stairs leading down to a huge, dark room.

I moved to climb down the stairs, but she held up a hand to stop me.

"Not yet," she said. "This is just in case."

"In case of what?" I asked.

"In case they can't stop it."

"Stop what?" There was something I didn't know, and, as much as I tried, I was getting nowhere. It was frustrating. I wanted to be included, too. I did not like being in the dark.

She sighed, exasperated, but not as much as I was. "Look, I'm not sure if you're allowed to know this, but you are, technically, a trainee now, and you won't shut up, so I'll tell you. That cloud-grid-thing you saw out the window? That was a group of sphormites. And if you thought those were bad, just wait until you see a sphorm."

"What's a—"

"Let me finish. A sphorm is what happens when all those clouds come together. They make one giant, spherical cloud that sinks over the city. It pours like crazy, and I've heard that, when lightning strikes during a sphorm, it creates magical fires that don't go out with water. You have to wait for the sphorm to clear, and by that time, everything is a mess. It's the magic's extremely unhelpful way of warning us when the Darkened make a major achievement."

"The Darkened? What's that supposed to mean?" Somehow, I was more confused than I had been *before* Viola had started explaining.

"Oh, that's right. You're new. The Darkened are the people who've lost touch with their light. They're just… born like that—evil. The worst part is that most manipulate the others around them into thinking that they are good. It's awful. See the Darkened only care about one thing: power, so they try to spread Darkness into other people. They don't really think at all, they just Darken."

"Wow, that's a lot to hear on my first day." I wasn't sure what else to say. It was my first day, and things were already going horribly wrong. A terrible storm was headed our way. I was beginning to think that maybe I couldn't handle the pressure this job put on me.

"Oh, yeah, it was a lot for me, too," she laughed.

"But don't worry. One person can easily stop a spho-rm. Especially Emery. He has the strongest connec-tion out of us all."

"So you're telling me that all of the dramatic stuff you just told me can be canceled with a single spell?"

"Yeah, but seeing your reaction was funny." Noticing my face, she added, "Oh, relax. They did it to Cyrus and I on our first day, too."

Suddenly, the speaker on the ceiling crackled, and I heard Sapphire's voice. "Red City is down! Distress signal received. They put up a huge fight, but lost. That's why the sphorm is so big. That's Red for you!"

"Oh, that's definitely Red," Viola agreed. "Cyrus knows their main lead. He knows too many people." She added the last part with a smirk.

It was interesting how close the leads seemed to be. I'd always imagined the government as a bunch of people in suits, speaking like the essays we had to write for school, but here I was, in the skyscraper, watching the leads make jokes over the speaker. They wore casual clothing, passed annoying chores (such as dealing with me) to one another, and, most importantly, seemed to have mutual respect for one another. I realized that they were more friends than coworkers. Even the other employees I'd seen were friendly with each other. *Powerless or not, I'm glad I finally got the position. I like this place.*

Before I could respond to Viola, another voice, this time concerned, came through the speaker. "I need all leads to the East Balcony. *Now.*"

It was Emery.

The mischievous smile was wiped off of Viola's face instantly and replaced with a worried, wide-eyed expression that made me hope I got out alive. "Wait here," she said, and started running toward the elevators.

"Hey, what? Wait!" I called after her.

She continued running, ignoring me.

"Viola, what was that announcement about?" I insisted.

"Look, he said '*now.*' " As she spoke, she pressed the button to open the elevator door. Being me, I followed her as fast as I could, though I wasn't fast enough, and the door closed in my face.

Fine, then. I turned towards the stairs. Running up, I began to wonder why I really cared so much? Was all this running worth it? Why did I need to know what happened?

Because this is my chance, I realized, *and I'm not about to just give it up. East balcony. That's the glass door I saw on the first day.*

I eventually reached the East Balcony in time to see Rose performing a spell, presumably the one to clear the sphorm. I watched her lift the prism from Adella's interview, line it up with the sphorm in the very center, and keep it there for a few seconds, staring at it. When it did nothing, she handed it back to Emery, shaking her head. Already, I could see a couple of raindrops start to fall outside.

"Why isn't it working, though?" Cyrus asked desperately.

"I don't know!" Sapphire cried, sounding somewhat crazy. "And I always know! I'm always right!

But this time, the facts just don't line up. I don't know and I don't like…" she trailed off as her dark blue eyes fell on me. I saw her face turn from confusion to understanding, and it made me uneasy. "That's it," she breathed. "You're the one thing that changed."

7

Sphorm Shelter

"Me? What's that supposed to mean?"

"You're the change," Sapphire repeated. "And if prisms can be broken only by nearby Darkness… but you don't act very Darkened… Again, I don't know…"

"Everybody, calm down," Emery said. Then he turned to me, "Do you have something to explain, Zia?"

"What? No! Of course not!" I said.

Thunder boomed from the rapidly advancing clouds, which, by then, were already spiraling into the sphorm.

"All right. We're getting nowhere, and those

clouds are getting closer. Rose, take Grandma Marigold with you and bring everyone in the skyscraper into the shelter. Except Adella. Cyrus, you go find her. She has the strongest connection in the entire city. Viola, gather the city and lead them to all the entrances to the shelter. And you," he turned to me, "get to the shelter *now*. We'll figure this out later."

I nodded and turned to walk away, fearing that rebellion might make the leads suspect me of being Darkened, or evil, or whatever they thought. *He just told Viola to bring* everyone in the city *into the shelter, and the shelter's a part of the skyscraper*, I thought. *This must really be serious.* As scared as I was, I continued on my way to the elevator, determined to convince everyone that I could be trusted. The minute the doors opened, I ran for the shelter.

I darted down the staircase, wishing that I'd brought a flashlight or a lantern or even a candle. Most people take their vision for granted. I was one of them. I stopped as my arm brushed against the cold, rough stone wall and the strange bricks started to glow. It was a similar glow to the green sign I'd seen on Emery's office door. Almost magical. It probably was. Some kind of magic, touch-activated walls. *Huh, that's pretty cool*, I thought, watching the light slowly fade away. I put my hand on the wall again, and kept it there as I wandered through the seemingly endless stone hallways.

My mind was running faster than ever before. *What's going to happen to me? Are the leads going to be able to stop the sphorm? What about my parents? What are they going to do when they find out I'm already in danger? And it's a kind of danger that even* Sapphire *can't explain. (From what I understood, Sapphire was the smartest of the leads.) All she said was "you're the change". What's that even supposed to mean? Does she think I caused it or somethi...*

I understood, then, what she meant. Sapphire was blaming me for deactivating the prism, our only way to clear the sphorm. *I* was what put us all in danger. And, worst of all, there was no way to disprove her theory. Maybe I *was* Darkened and didn't know it.

Was that even possible? All I knew was that we were all probably going to die, and it was my fault.

I looked down at my hands, reflecting miserably on all the trouble I had caused. *Great job, me. I should've listened on the first day. I should've left and not come back. Why do I always need to have it my way? Why am I so selfish? I should never have come here. If I was meant for magic, the leads would've known. I don't deserve magic. I was born powerless for a reason.*

I stopped, leaned on the wall, and started to cry. Great. Now I was feeling sorry for myself. Just more proof that I was selfish. As soon as the sphorm ended—if it ever did—I would resign, go home and never, ever come back.

"I should leave the magic to the real heroes," I whispered to myself. Real heroes like the leads, like Adella, like everyone else in the building. *Real* heroes with *real* power to make *real* changes. In other words, not me.

Suddenly, I became conscious of a constant metallic scratching sound echoing through the room. As if I hadn't just been sobbing uncontrollably about not being worthy, I wiped my tears and followed the sound.

Scrape, scrape, scrape.

I turned right.

Scrape, scrape.

Then left.

Scrape, scrape, scrape, scrape.

Then right again. I reached a wall, and the scratching was coming from just around the corner. The sound was like nails on a chalkboard, and I was somewhat scared, but I wasn't about to run away. I needed to find out what it was.

I'm breathing too loud, I thought, trying not to make a sound. I slowly lifted my hand off the wall to make sure that whatever was making the strange sound wouldn't see the bright white light. I tiptoed slowly to the corner, trying my hardest not to make a noise.

"Stupid lock," a very familiar and very unexpected voice muttered.

Oh, it's just—, I started to think, walking openly now to the person. Then, I realized that Adella, who was still a *trainee*, was picking the lock on a door marked "Leads Only".

With a final scrape, she was able to push the door open.

8

Raging Sphorm

"Hey, what are you do—" I started to say.

She turned and saw me. I could see no remorse in her eyes, just unbreakable, angry determination. "Don't interfere." She pulled a dagger out of the crossbody bag she was wearing.

"I thought we were friends," I said, in shock. "Why are you doing this? Wait… you're one of them?"

She turned away into the room, and I followed her. I couldn't believe that someone I had trusted as a friend had just betrayed me *and* everyone else in the skyscraper. But why? What did she gain by hurting others? Then, I remembered what Viola had told me earlier: the Darkened were brainwashed, blinded by the urge to just Darken others.

Inside, she was breaking a glass frame on the wall. As it shattered, a sheet of paper, yellowed with age, fell out. She snatched it and tried to run out the door.

Forgetting that she was armed, I blocked the exit. "Put it back."

"This isn't your place to save the world," Adella sneered.

"I'm not saving the world. I'm doing the right thing."

"You don't know anything."

"I know that breaking in and stealing are both crimes, Adella."

She lifted the dagger. "I already told you, 'don't interfere.' "

"You don't have to hurt me. Put the dagger away," I said.

"I will have to hurt you if you don't listen to me!"

"I don't have to obey a traitor." In anger, blindness in the dark, and hope of saving the leads from danger, I hit both my hands against the doorframe, and a bright flash of light flooded the room.

The sudden light shocked my traitorous "friend" into dropping the paper she'd been trying to steal, and I hurriedly picked it up. Then, I *ran*.

I ran through the dark hallways, back the way I'd come, to the entrance and out. I ran into the elevator, frantically pushed the button for the top floor, and let out a breath of relief as the doors closed. Though there was no sign that Adella was chasing me, I still felt safer in the elevator, far, far away from her dagger.

So it was her, I thought. She *is the Darkened one that broke the prism.* I couldn't wait to tell Sapphire and prove her theory wrong. I hadn't broken the prism. I hadn't put us all in danger. It was hilarious to think that someone would actually believe that kind of a theory!

When the elevator doors reopened, I ran out into the hallway and turned right just in time to watch

Emery through the glass door. He tried performing the spell one last time, as the rain started to pour heavily. Rose, who'd apparently finished her task of gathering everyone into the shelter, was there too, yelling for him to just come inside and let the sphorm continue. He ignored her, centering the prism on the sphormite in the middle, which had already started to merge with its companions into a sphorm. After keeping it like that for a moment, he gave up and brought it back down.

"I should be able to do this," came his muffled voice from outside.

"It's not your fault," Rose shouted. They both had to yell to be heard over the raging sphorm. "The prism's clearly broken."

"Let me just try one more time!"

She knocked the prism out of his hand and pulled him back inside, where they both saw me, standing in the hallway watching.

"You? I thought I told to you get in the shelter! Do you *want* to die?" Emery shouted over the crashing thunder.

"No! I came to tell you there's a traitor!" I yelled in reply.

"A traitor? Who?" said Rose.

Before I could respond, lightning struck the balcony. I knew what I had to do.

"I'm going," I announced.

"Going *where*? And who's the traitor?" Rose insisted.

Before either could stop me, I bolted towards the balcony door, determined to save everyone. I may not have started this like everyone thought, but I could stop it. I could make a real impact, and that was all I wanted.

I pushed open the door with all the force inside my body and ran outside. The rain poured onto me, soaking me in an instant and blurring my vision. The wind screamed, blowing a bit of my long, brown hair from behind me to in front of me, and into my face. My shoes were uncomfortably wet. Everything was cold and fast and loud.

Looking down onto the flooded floor, I spotted the prism. It was already half-submerged in water. The sphorm was so horrible, I was scared that the skyscraper would collapse. I picked up the prism. I tried to remember what Emery had done to perform the spell. He'd lifted the prism. I lifted it. He'd focused it on the center sphormite. By the time I had made it onto the balcony, the sphorm was almost entirely formed, so I just focused the prism on the center of it and hoped for the best. Then, he'd waited.

I stared through the prism into the dark clouds. *What now?* I thought. *Am I supposed to say something?*

"Uh… CLEAR THE SPHORM," I shouted. Nothing happened. "GET RID OF THE SPHORM!" Still nothing. "WORK!" I screamed. "WHY WON'T YOU JUST WORK? CLEAR! THE! SPHORM!"

Lightning struck behind me. I felt my back get very hot, then I smelled something burning. Thanks to Viola, I knew that the pouring rain would do nothing to put out the magical fire, so I chose to ignore my flaming hair.

It's not working. I'm going to die. And stupidly, too. I was never meant to be a hero, I thought.

"No," I said to myself, trying to ignore my annoyingly loud self-doubt. "I *CAN* do this."

Then, I saw white, and I felt my feet being lifted into the air. I saw trees, grass, mountains, and maybe a river flash by far, *far* below me, then I crashed onto the ground. Before I got the chance to even think, I felt exhaustion rush over me. I took a deep breath, then let myself drift off into sleep.

9

Post-Sphorm

I found myself awake, staring at a clear night sky scattered with stars. Beneath me was grass, and in my right hand, something small and cold was poking my palm. Staring into the stars, I tried to piece together what had happened. The last thing I remembered was... fear, but that wasn't all. I was happy too. For some reason, I remembered a feeling of triumph.

What had happened before that? I'd been accused of being Darkened by Sapphire, I remembered. How rude of her to say, when I'd—OH, YEAH—I'd saved everyone by clearing the sphorm (hopefully)! I'd discovered that Adella was a spy for the Darkened, ran up to inform the leads, then I'd had the genius idea to clear the sphorm. I'd seen a flash of land below me and I'd awoken here.

I sat up, still a little dazed. Strangely, I wasn't injured at all. You'd think that falling off of a balcony would hurt, but I was completely fine. My clothes, however, were another story completely. My favorite sweater was all ripped up. I was *missing a sleeve*.

"At least it wasn't your arm," I muttered to myself. Speaking of arms—or hands, really—I found that around my right hand, pieces of broken prism were scattered, and the sharp thing in my fist was the last remaining piece of Green city's prism. The leads were going to kill me. Lying next to my left hand was a crumpled, yellowed-with-age paper—the one Adella had been stealing. Seeing the paper led me to realize, *Shadows! I never told the leads who the traitor was! They probably still think it's me, and accidentally stealing the prism isn't going to do much to convince them otherwise. Great!*

I reached up and felt my hair. Everything, except for the part on my left that the wind had blown forward, was burned to just past shoulder length, and when I crumbled off the charred tips, it was slightly above my shoulders. I was more than a little disappointed. I'd been growing out my hair for years, but, standing up, I thought, *It's all worth it, to be a hero. I hope the city is safe now.*

I looked around. I was in a grass field, with forests on one side and the faraway outline of a city on the other. Cities on the planet Lucina were separated by thousands of miles of uninhabited land in order to ensure that the Darkened couldn't invade all of them at once. This land was called Midspace, and the only people you could find there were the Darkened, who were banned from entering cities.

Assuming that I'd been blown just out of Green City, I started towards the buildings, frowning as I spotted dark clouds over them.

So, I'm not really a hero, just an idiot, I thought, disappointed. However, as I approached the city, I realized that it was much larger than I had originally estimated, and it definitely wasn't the city Green.

Where was I?

As the suns rose, I spotted houses on the outskirts of the city, seemingly dull under the overcast sky. Walking deeper into the city, I noticed that everyone wore dull colors—gray, black, and muted brown. Not my style. The streets were littered with empty bottles, wrappers, and other types of trash, the walls of the buildings covered in graffiti. Any interaction between people consisted of yelling and the exchange of unkind language.

Once, a man bumped into another walking in the opposite direction.

"Get out of my way!" shouted the first man.

"Watch where you're walking," the other retorted.

"No, *you* watch where *you're* walking." The argument continued like this for about ten minutes as I hurried away, hoping not to end up in a similar situation.

Another time, a woman tripped over a piece of trash on the street, and began shouting curses at strangers passing by. The passersby weren't necessarily very kind either. Multiple jeered at the woman.

Overall, the place was cold and unfriendly and I didn't like it one bit. I tried my best to avoid the people walking past me. *I'm scared*, I thought. *Why did I come in here? I saw that it wasn't Green. What am I going to do? Well, a hero should be brave, and I want to be a hero, right? But how can I be brave when everyone here is so horrible?*

To this, even my optimistic Yellow part had nothing to say. As if the universe wanted to make my fear even worse, a boy, black-haired and blue-eyed, about my age, and a little taller, gave me a weird look.

Oh, no. Here comes an argument, I thought. Panic began building up inside of me.

"This place is not safe," he said quietly.

"Yeah, I can tell," I said, trying to act like I wasn't scared. "What do you want with me?"

"Relax, I'm not going to hurt you. I'm probably the only person you can trust in this city."

"And why, exactly, should I trust you?" I questioned, unconvinced.

10

Unexpected Friend

He glanced around, making sure no one was looking, then held up his hand, which was glowing a faint
red and said, "This."

About a week ago, I'd been pounding on the door
to the skyscraper, demanding, again, to be hired. As
Rose opened the door, I had caught a glimpse of
Emery and Adella behind her. He was showing her a
hand, glowing faintly green, and explaining that she
would soon learn how to make her own hand glow.

So this stranger was a magical. And he said that
he was 'the only person' I could trust. Which meant...
"Everyone else here is Darkened, then?" I was still
scared, but, as far as I could tell, he meant it when he

said he could be trusted.

He nodded. "Nobody knows about me, so please don't tell. Though, you're pretty clearly a foreigner, aren't you?"

"Yeah," I said. Now that I knew he was magical, and very powerful as well, with the way he could make his hand glow, I knew that he might be someone who could help me get home.

"Archer Red," he introduced himself, smiling. "Nice to meet you."

"Zia Allight." We shook hands. "So, I guess I must have ancestors from there."

"Allight? That's ironic. Do you know what city this is?"

"But Allight's not Darkened," I said, confused. Allight, the largest city on the planet, couldn't be Darkened. During my time visiting the skyscraper, I'd learned that there was a communicator in each city. When a city was taken over, it automatically sent a distress signal, then self-destructed, as had happened in the city of Red. Allight's communicator was still working.

"Yeah, it is, clearly. Has been for the past three years. They took over when I was ten," he informed me. "It's a messy place, but it was a nice change from the way we used to camp out every night in the Midspace. I can tell you firsthand that sleeping on dirt and grass for ten years is in no way good for your back."

I was too shocked to even think about how casually Archer had mentioned that he'd once lived in the Midspace. From what I'd seen, the Midspace was a huge field with nothing but grass and more grass. Sure, it was pristine, untouched wildlife, but my eyes were getting tired of the color green, which is not to say that Allight was a preferable sight to see.

"But how can I be in Allight? That would mean I traveled thousands of miles and crossed the North Golden Rivers."

"You WHAT?"

"I'm from Green."

"How did you get here?"

"Well, it started when my friend from school,

Adella—"

"Oh, not *her*," Archer whined.

"You know Adella?"

"Yeah, and I honestly wish I didn't. Did she stab you in the back too?"

"Wow, you too, huh?"

"She and I were the only two non-Darkened people in our group. We were maybe six or seven years old. My connection is too strong to be dimmed, and she had a friend to keep her happy. That would be me. Obviously, no one knew we weren't Darkened. Out of nowhere, she disappeared one day. During that time, I came up with this idea that we should try to stop the Darkened from the inside. By the time I saw her again, and tried to tell her about my idea, she was one of them."

"Wow. So she's always been a terrible person," I said.

"Whatever, she's irrelevant. You continue your story," he replied.

I told him the rest of my story—how I'd been denied the job until the sphorm, discovered Adella was a traitor, and tried to clear the sphorm—and, by the time I'd finished, the two of us had concluded that the magic must've pitied me, and blasted me out of the way of the sphorm before it could kill me.

"Well, we have to do something," I said. "We can't just let this happen."

"Agreed. I think we should join forces. The more, the merrier—or stronger, I guess, in this case."

"Not like I'm very strong, being powerless and all, but deal."

"So, I'll pretend that you're a new recruit that I met on a trip outside the city," said Archer. "But if you're going undercover, those ripped clothes won't be very helpful. Not to mention how colorful they are. We have a whole 'no color' policy here, for obvious reasons. Let's go steal you a disguise."

"*Steal?*"

"This is literally a city of *evil*. It's the norm."

11

A Start to Victory

"Are you sure we can just take them?" I asked for the hundredth time, pulling out the few cubes of searock (the Lucinian currency; it doesn't actually come from the sea, but it's a very strong, bluish-gray metal that we cut into cubes) from the pocket of my old pants. I was currently wearing a plain white shirt and black pants. The lack of color was not something I enjoyed, but it would help me stay undercover and that was what mattered. We'd also stolen some wire and string and used them to turn the shard of the prism into a necklace.

"I promise, and anyway, we're paying the owner back by saving the city, right?" Archer reassured me.

"I guess," I agreed reluctantly, throwing away my old, ripped clothes. *Sacrifices must be made*, I thought.

Leaving the empty store, I began to wonder what we'd do next. I'd only ever *dreamt* of saving a city, never *actually done it*. I hadn't realized just how much planning heroes had to do. I'd assumed heroes just always knew what to do. I now realized what a stupid thought that had been. "So, where do you think we should start?" I asked, hoping Archer had some ideas.

"I say we use the communicator to ask for help from the other cities. I have experience with it." He smirked at the last sentence.

"What do you mean, 'experience?' "

"Why do you think there was never a distress message? And do you remember that unexplained storm that was all over the news? It wasn't just any storm, it was a sphorm. That was when they took over Allight. I just shut down the machine before the signal could be sent. I didn't really want to do it, of course, but I had to make sure they thought I was one of them."

"Oh! That's smart! Why didn't you do that for the city of Red?"

"I was the only one smart enough to figure out that the machines send distress signals in emergencies, and I wasn't there."

"But, I thought the Darkened were all sinister and evil masterminds."

"Some of them," he said. Then, there are those idiots who are entirely incapable of doing anything. They just *allow* themselves to be brainwashed."

"That's not the nicest word choice," I commented.

"Some people don't deserve the nicest word choice," Archer replied.

"I can't argue with that," I shrugged.

12

Sad People, Bad People

"Identification?" demanded the frowning guard at the door to the Darkened skyscraper. He was tall, and looked as if he could easily beat ten of me in a fight. Looking around, I could see that the walls seemed to be made of the same stone as the one back home, though the bricks didn't have that strange, glowing, fluid quality.

"You know *exactly* who I am," Archer responded.

"Identification?" He repeated in the same, irate voice.

Archer grudgingly handed him a card.

The guard studied the card, then eyed me angrily. "And for her?"

"She's with me," Archer responded briefly.

"I need identification," the guard insisted again, raising his already loud voice.

"She's a new recruit. She doesn't have a card," Archer lied smoothly.

"What, am I supposed to trust you like some suns hine light one?" the guard snapped.

'Suns hine light one?' Is that supposed to be an insult? I thought.

"Yeah," Archer retorted. " 'Cause you *are* one. Weak and light. Now, let us through, or else."

"*I'm* weak? You're what? Seven years old?"

"Thirteen."

"Same difference," the guard laughed. It was the most unfriendly laugh I'd ever heard. It almost made me lose all hope that we could fix the city. "You're a little kid."

"Do you know who I am?" Archer asked, clearly trying to keep calm. I didn't blame him. This guard had no respect for anyone but himself.

"Some kid."

"Actually, I'm in charge of the communicator. I'm willing to bet you've never hacked into a communicator and blocked the distress message so that the other cities wouldn't find out we took over."

The guard silently and reluctantly let us through, glaring at us venomously. He knew he'd lost the argument.

" 'Weak and light?' " I repeated to Archer once the guard was out of earshot.

"Sorry. It's an insult here. Probably our rudest one. I hate it too. Magicals are way stronger than the Darkened, realistically. This planet isn't the best for making weapons, so magic's a huge advantage. Plus, I've heard rumors that say on Ea—"

"You had to use the *rudest insult* just to be allowed into a building?" I interrupted in disbelief.

"Yeah. That guy knew *exactly* who I was, too. He just wanted to win. That's how all interactions go here. You're probably the first person in months or even years to not be like that to me."

"You're kidding." I was shocked. How could people live in such a cold, unfriendly place, without any positive human interaction? That would be my Orange side speaking. "Even your parents are like this?"

"My parents wouldn't care if I *died*. They'd be too busy being awful to people, like they always are. But most of the Darkened aren't really bad. There are two types of them: Corrupt and Sad. The Corrupt are born like that, self-absorbed and evil. They just want to cause pain. But, the Sad are just… sad. Broken, I guess. They lost their light somehow in their past.

"That guard at the door? He always wants to be better than people, since, growing up, his older brothers were 'better' than him, according to their parents. Don't ask how I know. People talk here. But anyway, when you don't love yourself or your life, it's pretty hard to love others."

"Wow. I thought they were all just born evil," I said, processing the new information. According to Viola, the Darkened were terrible monsters that wanted to ruin the world, but maybe the leads didn't know about the Sad.

"Some are, but again, most are Darkened through their environment. Bad parents, unfair rules, loneliness—things like that."

"They're not really evil, then." Surely, if these people hadn't been born Darkened, they didn't have to die that way... "We need to save them, too," I declared.

13

Loyal Traitor

"So, you've just been monitoring the communicator the whole time?" I asked. We had made our way to the room with the communicator.

"Yup. I know my way around it," Archer replied.

"Why didn't you just call for help earlier, then?"

"Because, once help arrived, everyone would know it was me who called the other cities. I'd be alone in a city of merciless, evil beings until the other cities were prepared to help, and I don't know any spells. Speaking of which, I know you're powerless and all, but do you happen to have *overheard* any spells? I was hoping you could teach me some."

"Sure, if I remember them," I said. Then, I remembered something else. Something much more important. The paper that Adella had been stealing. It was still in my hand. I never had read what was on it. It had been slightly crumpled, but I did my best to smooth it out on top of the large, rectangular communicator.

"What is that?" Archer asked.

"No idea, but a certain mutual backstabber of ours was in the process of stealing it," I replied.

"Must be important, then," Archer said. "You read it, I'll send the message for help."

"To which city?"

"All of the light ones. We're going to need a *lot* of help to take back Allight."

I began to skim over the paper silently. It described light magic of all colors, and how the magic worked. Then, I reached the page number. 4/513. "There's 512 more of these!" I exclaimed, looking up. My curiosity was sparked. Where were the rest? *What* were the rest? I handed the paper to Archer. "I'll take over sending the message."

As I touched the keyboard to type the message, though, the screen went all white. "What did I do?" I asked, startled, as I lifted my hands.

Archer looked at the screen. "Nothing, it's probably just a glitch. Give it a minute and it'll go back to normal."

Just as he had predicted, the screen flickered back to normal in a few seconds, but a message popped up. "Error—message over fifteen characters. Error—can only send to one recipient at a time."

When Archer couldn't fix the glitch, we settled on sending the message to Green, since they knew me, and writing, "Help. City Dark. Zia." Once we clicked send, the screen flashed white and read "refreshing." We figured the leads would be happy to know I was safe, and would send help fast. What we didn't expect, however, was to hear a crash a few hours later, go outside to explore, and find a flyercraft with a green stripe on the tail—the mark of Green city—right in front of the skyscraper.

The pilot exited. We both knew her.

14

Hide, Seek, and Redemption

I turned toward Archer. "Is it her, or am I seeing things?"

"No, it's definitely her."

We backed up into the lobby, leaving the door slightly open so we could see out of it.

"What do we do?"

"Nothing for now. She's not—Oh. Scratch that. She is."

Looking out the small crack between the door and wall, I realized that Adella was walking towards the skyscraper. Towards us.

Think of something, I pleaded my brain. *Have a genius idea! Be smart, like the heroes you read about!*

And do it fast! Glancing around, I noticed that Archer was wearing a black jacket tied around his waist. "Give me that jacket."

"What? Why?"

"Just do it. She's coming."

He took it off and handed it to me, and I put it on as Adella neared the door. I pulled the hood over my head and kept my face toward the ground. "Let's go," I whispered. We started towards the door, the guard from earlier glaring at us as we exited.

It went well… up until just outside the door when my plan backfired. I should've figured.

Adella recognized Archer. "Archer," she called, smiling.

"What do you want with me?" he answered, stopping. The tone of voice Archer used sounded exactly like my current thoughts, though, for obvious reasons, I couldn't speak my mind.

"Wait, I need you to listen," she pleaded.

"You didn't listen to me, so why do you expect me—"

"I've changed my mind!"

"Right," he scoffed. "When *I* ask for help, it's 'Are you kidding? I'm part of the better ones now', but when *you* need help, I have to come to the rescue. *NO.*"

"Really! I made a friend, and she changed my point of view. She cared, and wanted to help, even though she was powerless."

Powerless? Was she talking about *me*? *I* changed her point of view? No, of course not. She'd stolen a flyercraft and taught herself to pilot it, just to reach Allight. I could never influence someone like that.

"Oh?" said Archer dryly, still skeptical. "Then why are you here? Go back and be with your new friend. Go away."

Ignoring his rude remark, Adella responded eagerly. "The communicator in Green got a message… with her name in it. We'd all assumed she was dead, the way she cleared that sphorm! I wasn't even there, but the ones who were… they were shocked!"

I cleared the sphorm? I thought excitedly, slowly

realizing that she *was* talking about me. The way she's talking, it's like I'm a *hero*. I'm not a hero. I'm a nobody. *A nobody that cleared a sphorm*, sang a voice in the back of my head. I couldn't deny it was telling the truth.

I lifted my head, completely forgetting that my "disguise" depended on me facing the floor. "You talking about me?" I smiled smugly.

"Zia! Look, I'm sorry about the stealing. I wasn't myself, spying on the government. I was brain-washed, but now I'm back on the good side, and I'm ready to help!" said Adella.

"You mean 'good side' as in 94.7 percent Blue?" I laughed. I was feeling optimistic suddenly, and that always came hand-in-hand with a little mischief.

"No, I mean good side as in 74.3 percent Orange," Adella responded.

"Well, '94.7 percent Blue,' welcome to the team," I said.

"Blue. I like that nickname," said Archer. To my relief, he no longer seemed upset, and was open to forgiving Adella (Blue). Of course, some teasing over the whole Blue thing was going to be involved, but I'd be a part of that as well.

"Yeah," I agreed. "So very fitting and extremely definitely true."

"So true that the words blue and true even rhyme," he noted.

"Oh, yeah. It's meant to be."

"Come on, you guys. Forget the past, it's history," Adella (now Blue) laughed.

"No, I don't think that I will," I smiled.

"You will always be Blue to us," Archer added.

15

The Greater Plan

"So, how come you're the one they sent?" I asked. As far as the leads knew, Adella (Blue) was a newbie to magic, completely unable to control it. Plus, she was under the age of sixteen. Here on Lucina, sixteen is the adult age. Once an individual turns sixteen, he or she can legally buy a house, live alone, and pilot a flyercraft. Then, I added, "No offense, I mean."

"Oh," she smirked. "They didn't send me."

"Of course," said Archer, shaking his head in teasing disapproval. "Had to be a traitor one last time and run away. And with an entire flyercraft, as well."

"Shut up," countered Blue. "You'd do it too."

She got no response.

"Guys, focus," I said. "Blue, when's help from home coming?"

"Uh… it's not."

"What? But we sent the message. Did they not get it?" I asked.

"Did *you* not show them? What happened?" Archer continued.

"No, no, I didn't do anything! They saw your name on it and immediately dismissed the message. The leads thought that A) you were a traitor anyway. It was all probably part of a trick or a plan, or B) you most likely hadn't survived the blast and it was a co-incidence. I tried to convince them that you could have miraculously survived, but it clearly didn't work, so I just stole the flyercraft and followed a map —also stolen—here," Blue explained.

"Where'd you learn to fly, anyway?" Archer asked. Now that he said it, I was curious as well. Surely the Darkened didn't teach her *that* as well.

"I taught myself," she proclaimed proudly.

"It shows," he muttered.

"*You* have absolutely no right to speak here. *You've* never flown a flyercraft," Blue retorted, a smug smile on her face.

"Well, at first glance, it would look like you haven't either."

"You two! We have more serious things to think about than Blue's horrible piloting skills!"

"Hey! I'm *not* horrible!"

I ignored her interruption, choosing not to point out that she was wrong. "Listen. We're three kids, alone, in a city of evil, trying to do the impossible and take it back. How are we ever going to have a *chance* of success?"

"We could always send a distress message to the other cities," Blue suggested. "And just leave the work to the adults."

"Yeah. Adults who can actually *fly* flyercrafts, not crash them," said Archer.

"Sure," I agreed, filled with hope at the thought of actually being able to take back the city, but more than a little disappointed, knowing that I wouldn't do any of the work myself. I wouldn't be the hero of the story, the savior of the city. *But the city will be bright again*, I reminded myself. *That's what matters.* Not *who does it.*

"But we'd have to wait a little. The machine's refreshing or whatever. I couldn't fix it," Archer pointed out.

"Oh. That may be a problem." Blue frowned.

"Why's it a problem?" asked Archer. "It's not like we have a time limit or anything."

"You haven't heard?" Blue responded, surprised. "My parents told me a few weeks ago, when the government hired me."

"As Blue," Archer and I interrupted simultaneously.

"Yeah, yeah. As Blue," Blue sighed. "But really. The Great Plan? No one told you?"

He shook his head.

"Well no one told *me*, obviously, so keep going," I said, unnecessary as it may have been.

"They're spreading the Darkness. Now that Red's been taken, there are three Darkened cities: Red, Al-light, and Purple, twenty years ago. One more city and the Darkened have the majority of the continent. And they plan to get that last city a week from now. My test scores were always fake. They always had me lie on the surveys, just to build up the lie of being 94.7 percent Blue. They had me dress in blue on the interview day, and on most days that I went to the skyscraper. They never told me, but this plan had been in place all along. I wasn't just spying, I was helping to complete the Great Plan."

We spent a few moments in anxious silence, all three of us worrying about the task we were facing. In the span of a week, we would have to find a way to stop a plan that had been in place for seven years, maybe even more, and carry out our counter-plan. This was bigger than any pop-quiz, any final exam, any major project I'd ever done in my life. Thinking back on all the times I'd thought problems like wanting closer friends were serious, I almost laughed.

Now, I had bigger things to think about. But I knew that, no matter what happened, I would find a way. *We* would find a way. Determined and hopeful through the worry, I declared, "They may have their Great Plan, but we'll make a Great*er* Plan!"

16

A Dilemma

"The only way is to fight them," insisted Archer as he, Blue, and I were gathered around his father's desk in his house, trying to create an organized plan.

"Fight them and *kill* them? They may be evil, but we're not. How could we kill them?" I countered.

"What do I write, then?" asked Blue. The three of us had agreed that Blue, who had the neatest handwriting, should write out our plan.

"Nothing, yet. We need to find another way."

She nodded, but Archer resisted. "Zia, there's nothing else we can do."

"There has to be. Killing would make us evil instead of turning them good. That's the opposite of what we want."

"Whoa, who said we're making them good?" he asked.

"What else are we going to do? Throw them back out into the Midspace so that it can all happen again? No, we have to re-Brighten them."

"First of all, that's not how conquering works. Conquering happens through battles and fights. That means killing. Second, how do you even plan to re-Brighten them? That's never happened before."

"Hello! Yes, it has. I'm back to my old self, aren't I?" Blue pointed out.

"Yeah, see! I changed her. I'll change them all."

"Changing her was a process that took months. How long do you think befriending everyone in the city and giving them free therapy is going to take? Plus, she was Darkened through sadness. We have no way of really knowing how everyone else was Darkened," Archer said.

"But there has to be a way. There *has* to be. I refuse to kill people."

"Wait," Blue said abruptly. "My former commander told me about magic in preparation for spying a few years ago! Something about how some old farts from the past knew the secret to all kinds of spells that don't involve battle!"

"Like…" I started.

"Like Brightening," she finished.

"Well, what's the secret?" I asked eagerly.

"I said the old farts knew, not me."

"Oh, come on!"

"You didn't let me finish. I know how to find out! Each city has one page of a book that we call *The Pages of Power* in a locked room in the sphorm shelter. We think that the leads of ancient times split up the book so that we—*the Darkened*—couldn't get to them all at once. That's actually what I was trying to steal before you had to jump in and be all heroic, Zia. 'I just want to do the right thing. Blah, blah, greater good.' "

"You're getting off topic," I laughed.

"Fine. The Darkened had known about the rooms

in the shelters for a while, but they only recently discovered the Pages when they developed a lock pick that could open the lock and found the ones at Allight. Obviously, being the most important city, it had the majority of the book: table of contents, Lucina's history, and the minor spells. The other cities each have one page, with the major information. Green's, for instance, has all the info about the magic types."

"She's right," I confirmed, remembering the paper that I'd squashed into the pocket of my pants. "So, we go to the shelter, find the pages, and see what we can find on Brightening."

I watched as Blue wrote this down on the paper, then, glancing at the window, I realized that the suns were setting. *Already? Wow, a hero's day goes by fast!* "Tomorrow," I added, and she scribbled that down too.

We ate whatever Archer could find in the nearly empty cabinets. The house may have seemed well-furnished and organized at first glance, but the cabinets were bare, the furniture almost never used. The house felt empty, like no souls lived inside.

During the night, we slept in the bunk bed in Archer's guest bedroom. Surprisingly to me, but not to him or Blue, we weren't discovered. Archer's parents were constantly gone, according to him, and didn't have time to check whether or not their son was plotting treason with friends.

I'm glad my parents aren't like that, I thought, lying in the top bunk and staring at the ceiling through the shadows. Suddenly, and not very much like a hero, I started to feel homesick. I was a kid. A powerless, helpless kid. What was I doing, saving a city thousands of miles away from my home back in Green? I realized that my parents didn't even know I was here.

What are they thinking now? What are they doing? Tears filled my eyes. *Are they worried? I wish I could tell them I'm safe... well, as safe as I can be in a city of Darkened, which is not very safe at all. Wow, was it really just yesterday morning that I was leaving the house, that Dad was trying to talk me out of it?*

Should I have listened to him? If I had, I'd be home right now. I'd be safe. I'm so selfish. I didn't even think about the dangers of being a hero, I just jumped into it because I wanted to. If I put myself in danger, potentially get hurt… maybe worse… I don't want to think about it… Mom and Dad would be so sad. They probably are *sad. The leads probably told them I blasted myself into pieces. I can't imagine how they feel right now. I wish Mom and Dad were here. I miss home. I want to go home. I promise never to jump into something like this again. I promise to listen next time… I hope there's a next time. I don't want to die because I did something dumb. I shouldn't have thrown myself into danger like this. I'm so stupid. What's my problem? Why do I only think about my-self? Why didn't I just listen to Dad, to the leads, to everyone? Why couldn't I just accept that I wasn't magical? Why do I always have to get my way? Why am I doing this? Why did I come here? Why did I think I could be a hero? Why did I think I could change anything? Why do I always have to be differ-*

ent and break the rules? Why? Why? Why?

At some point, between sobs and sniffles, I managed to fade into a restless sleep.

17

Swords and Whispers

I was fighting. Without a weapon. Without protection. Without skills. Without backup. And it was against five significantly tall Darkened people with swords. The swords seemed to be dripping with liquid, runny and black. I didn't know what it was, I just knew that it would kill me. Why was I here? We'd never agreed to kill them. What was going on?

I didn't have the time to ponder that, though, as the one closest to me slashed with his sword. I ducked, just in time to avoid a beheading, though a few strands of my hair, which had already been through so much, brushed against the dripping goo.

Another one slashed, and barely missed my neck.

I tried to run, but I was being held in place by fear. It felt like chains were wound around my entire body. I knew, deep down, they weren't there, but, no matter how much I tried, I just couldn't move.

"Stop, please," I yelled in desperation.

"You chose this," said one of the Darkened, the one who had first tried to decapitate me, in a whispery, echoey, eerie voice. The other four silently moved, floating along until I was in the center of a tightly guarded circle. Not that I could move anyway. I was still paralyzed with fear.

"You will perish," whispered one, in that same voice.

"Failure," said an overlapping whisper.

I glanced around myself, trying to find a way to escape.

"Powerless."

"Useless."

"Wannabe."

"Not special."

As the swords left gashes on my leg, my arm, my

face, my side, I realized that, for some odd reason, the whispers cut deeper than the blades.

"Hopeless."

"Worthless."

"Blue!" I called. "Archer! Help!" Nobody responded. I was all on my own.

Then, a sword came for my chest.

My eyes opened and I quickly tried to jump up from bed, forgetting that I'd chosen the top bunk. Ow. I was dripping with sweat and breathing so hard I thought the world could hear it.

"You good? That sounded painful," came a hushed voice from below me.

"Yeah," I whispered back shakily, trying to process where I was and what was going on. The swords... the whispers... where did they go? Was I dead? Was I in the hospital? Oh. They were dreams. "Bad dream, I think. What time is it?"

"About three in the morning," Blue responded.

"Why are you awake?" I asked. "We're supposed to explore the skyscraper at five!"

"I'm a night person and an insomniac. This always happens. Well, not the whole saving the world thing," she laughed. I'd known she was a late sleeper, but not *this* late. Though, I kind of understood. Sometimes, I'd get caught up reading a really good book and accidentally stay up until about three as well.

"Listen," I started. "I don't think I'm cut out for this. I'm—"

Blue cut me off. "For what?" she whispered.

"Saving the city—being a hero, that stuff. I'm a kid! A powerless, useless kid who can't change anything."

"As if, dummy! You changed *me*! Your 'I can do anything' mindset made me snap out of the darkness. *You* brought me back to the good side! You can do anything and everything. Trust me. I know firsthand."

"You're just saying it. I'm a wannabe. I'm an impulsive, selfish idiot."

"Say what you like, but keep in mind that your impulsive-idiotness cleared the sphorm that Emery, the *city's main lead*, the strongest guy in the sky-scraper, couldn't clear."

"So it worked?"

"Yeah! Believe me, Zia, you can do it, and I, as your self-proclaimed best friend, promise to be there every step of the way."

"Thanks," I smiled. Maybe I really could do something here. Maybe it was a good thing that I had gone to the skyscraper. After all, the only reason I had a best friend now was because I went. Maybe things weren't what they seemed to be… "But go to sleep, now. We have a long day ahead of us."

18

Not a Morning Person

In contrast to when my nightmares had woken me the night before, I slowly drifted awake. My eyes took in my surroundings. The morning light of the two suns shone bright on the white walls of the room through a window, bordered by old, gray, velvet curtains.

I climbed down from the top bunk. Pushing the door open, I walked to where I remembered Archer's bedroom to be. The night before we'd agreed to wake up by five, and if any of us hadn't, he or she would be woken up. Judging by the amount of light, it was well past five. I knocked on the wooden door, and it promptly opened to reveal a frowning face that confirmed my suspicions.

"Took you long enough," Archer muttered, shaking his head. "Do you even know what time it is?"

"What time?" I asked, my voice cracking after not being used for hours in a row.

Ignoring my question, he continued. "I knocked on your door for a good ten minutes before giving up and leaving."

"Oh, I was asleep. Guess I'm a deep sleeper."

"A very deep sleeper. Zia, it's nine o'clock," he said, exasperated. "And I assume Blue is still asleep?"

"Yup," I confirmed.

He sighed. "She's always been a ridiculously late sleeper. I wouldn't be surprised if she was up until three in the morning."

"So you're an early riser, then?"

"No, I'm a human being with a normal sleep schedule," Archer said disapprovingly.

"I'll go get her."

"Get up," I whispered.

"Go away," Blue mumbled, half—no, mostly—asleep.

"I told you you were up too late. We have to go."

"You're welcome for being your nightmare therapist. And on short notice, too."

"Oh, just get up. It's nine o'clock." I knew she was right, and I didn't feel like losing an argument so early in the morning. That would be my Red side speaking.

"Get up," she mocked sleepily. I could tell that she knew she was right. "It's nine—wait, it's NINE?"

"Yes, it is."

"So much for being early so no one's there." She sat up. "Well, we're already late. It won't hurt if I sleep a little longer," she added, laying back down.

"No—"

Then, we heard a loud knock on the door, followed by an annoyed "Hurry up!"

"Yeah," I said, loud enough that Archer could hear through the door that it was Blue being slow, not me. "Hurry up, Blue."

"Ugh, I was already awake anyway." Blue quickly jumped out of bed and opened the door.

"Morning," she smiled casually, as if she hadn't just overslept by four entire hours. I was glad that the blame was off of me.

While I smothered a laugh, Archer rolled his eyes.

19

Touch Activated?

We left the house, walked to the center of the city, and after another significantly rude exchange of words with the guard at the door, the three of us were allowed into the skyscraper. Since we'd come late, people were all over the place, shouting and arguing with one another. I was still fairly shocked about the amount of conflict in this city. The stone in the walls was the same, but the people... the people needed help. That was all I could think. Then I suddenly realized how awful it must have been for Archer and Blue to grow up in this alternate-dimension-like world. How hard it must have been for Archer to keep hoping, and how Blue *had* lost hope entirely. How they must have struggled to keep themselves and each other going. How everyone here must've struggled. Mostly, I pondered how different this place was from home, in the worst way possible. But now, we could be the ones to fix it. We were already the ones fixing it. Whether it took only us, or everyone in all the cities, we'd find a way to make it happen. We were saving not just the city, but the whole planet, from the Great Plan of the Darkened. We could make a change, and we were doing it right then and there. I'd always wanted to make a change.

Since the people of the past built all the sphorm shelters nearly identical, Blue had memorized the layout of the shelter in Allight in preparation for stealing from Green. According to her, the adults had made her practice "millions of times," and she claimed that it was "in no way a hyperbole. They really did! Well, at least it felt like they did." It didn't take long for Blue to remember which way the room containing the Pages was, and soon enough I started to recognize the hallways I'd followed the scraping noise through.

"These shelters really need some lighting," Blue commented. In the dark, I couldn't see her face, but from her voice alone I could tell that she was extremely annoyed.

I couldn't blame her. Who wouldn't be annoyed, wandering through the darkness for what felt like fore—oh, yeah. There *was* lighting! *Didn't she say that she's been through these hallways "millions" of times? How come she doesn't know about the walls? Oh, well. Guess I'll teach her today.* "They're touch activated," I explained. "See?" I brushed my fingertips against the wall and the same fluid glow lit up the wall and the room around it. My hand guided the light along the wall as I continued walking forward. The light seemed to flow and ripple over the wall. It was strange, but then, everything about these past few days had been strange in such an amazing way.

Blue and Archer stopped in their tracks simultaneously and stared at me, both wearing the same what-just-happened expression.

Slowly moving my hand off the wall, I said, "What? What are those faces for?"

"How did you do that?" Archer questioned.

"I… touched it." What was so confusing about touch-activated lights? It was a government building after all. The government was supposed to have cool, high-tech gadgets, weren't they?

"These walls have never done that before, and they didn't do that in Green either. Speaking of Green, by the way, how did you do that thing back there? The light flash?"

Light flash? Oh, she's talking about the thing where I hit those walls and they got bright, I thought. "I just hit my hands on the walls. I probably over-loaded the touch sensors, that's all," I explained, con-fused. How could the touch sensors work for only one person? Maybe it was because Blue was Darkened back then. Maybe the walls could somehow sense one's magic, and didn't light up for the Darkened.

"Zia, there *are* no touch sensors. I've brushed against these walls maybe thirty times already and nothing's lit up," Archer said.

I began to get nervous for some reason. What was going on? Were the sensors broken and glitching?

"Are you... hiding something?" he asked suspiciously.

"No, of course not!" I rushed to defend myself, though I stepped back slightly. "I... I'm sure it was the magic taking pity on me again or something. A girl born powerless. It must have felt bad and wanted to make powerless life more convenient." To be honest, I was mostly trying to convince myself. Though I knew better than anyone that I wasn't keeping any secrets, there was no better explanation, and I couldn't really blame Blue and Archer for distrusting me.

"I don't think she is. It doesn't sound like her. If she really was Darkened, I'd know," Blue backed me up. "Plus it wouldn't make sense that the walls only *light up* for one of *the Darkened*, you know?"

"True, but she could easily be hiding something else," Archer said.

"What is there for me to even be hiding?" I asked.

There was silence for a moment, as Archer and Blue pondered my question. I felt betrayed. Did they really, seriously think I was hiding something? All I wanted was to help. To my relief, however, neither could come up with any reasonable ideas.

"See? I'm not evil," I said.

Archer shrugged. "Yeah. You're probably right about the magic feeling bad. It's happened before with the whole unharmed-after-the-sphorm-blast thing."

Blue nodded in agreement.

"Plus, I went through all of those years of magic tests with no knowledge of the magic, so, unlike someone I know—Blue—I couldn't have been lying." I knew how silly I was being. Of course, I was sure that I wasn't Darkened, but part of me was scared of losing my new friends and my role as a hero, everything I'd been working up to for the past few days. *But I've done nothing wrong and nobody has anything against me. A glitch in the government's equipment will not lose me my friends, or my job*, I reminded myself. In my head, I laughed at myself a little. Some hero I was, scared of being taken down by light-up walls.

20

To Yellow We Go!

We continued through the rooms and hallways for a few more minutes, this time with a very helpful source of light, until we finally found the room we were looking for. The door, like almost everything else in this skyscraper, was identical to the door I'd seen in Green. It even had the same sign on it: "Leads Only! Persons Without Permit, Do Not Enter!"

"Blue, do you still have that lock pick they gave you?" Archer asked.

"Shadows! You just reminded me! I forgot it back in Green! I know exactly where it is too! I left it at my house," she replied.

In the dim light emitted by the wall, the piece of

broken prism on my neck glinted dramatically, and it caught my eye. "Will this work?" I asked, taking off the makeshift necklace.

"Maybe." Blue took the shard of prism from my hand and twisted it around in her fingers, examining it. She started to pick the lock.

"How come they taught *you* all the cool skills?" Archer asked Blue.

"I'm a spy, and you're a nobody," she replied smoothly.

I smothered a laugh and, just before Archer could answer Blue's rude remark, the door to the room with Allight's Pages of Power creaked open. We had done it.

The room itself was identical to the one in Green, but inside lay an overturned desk, made of wood that looked so old it could've been the desk of someone who'd lived on Earth. Around the desk and all over the floor, shards of shattered glass lay scattered on the floor—the remains of the glass case where the Pages must've been held—and a box with a keyhole sat in the right-hand corner.

Blue removed the shard of prism from the door and, though we were all wearing shoes, carefully avoided the glass while making her way to the box. "I'm going to try it here, too," she said, and she started to pick the lock. "It's not like it can really be used to focus light anymore."

To my surprise, after a few minutes of scratching and picking, the lid of the box popped open, and when we lifted it, we found all the pages we'd expected to find, including the table of contents:

Table of Contents

"Major Spells might include something about

Brightening," Archer pointed out.

"Okay, if Types of Magic, the one we found in Green, is number four, then Major Spells, number three, should be found in the city of Yellow, going in the order of light on a spectrum," I reasoned .

"Makes sense," Blue agreed.

"To Yellow, we go!" I declared.

"I'll fly us!" Blue suggested with a smirk.

"I don't think so," said Archer.

"You got any better ideas?"

21

In Yellow We Are!

"So, Yellow isn't also secretly Darkened, is it?" I laughed, strapping myself in a seat of the half-crashed flyercraft that Blue had reassured us "definitely still worked."

"Very funny," said Archer. "But I think the real question is 'Blue, have you ever taken flying lessons?' "

"That's a great question! No, I have not, but I got to Allight, didn't I?"

"You *crashed*!" he shouted in reply.

"Ah, just trust me!" she exclaimed, clearly struggling to find the power switch.

"Right, yes, let's just trust the traitor, shall we?"

"*Ex*-traitor," she corrected.

"Maybe *I* should fly it," I suggested, trying to look like I was serious. "I've broken a prism *and* possibly a communicator. I mean, how many more things can one person break?"

"Yeah, no," Archer smiled. "I guess Blue's the best option then."

"Of course I am."

She eventually found the power button, and we took off, joking around too much to care about the dangers we would soon face. It might've been the first time since Blue had told us about the Great Plan that we'd all felt free of our worries.

We arrived in Yellow about four hours later, all three of us more than ready to escape the cramped space inside the flyercraft. Somehow, miraculously, the flight had been relatively smooth, not counting some turbulence, and one time when Blue, overly confident in her flying skills, had tried to fly in a loop-de-loop, and we'd plummeted down. We would've crashed into the ground, had she not quickly brought the flyercraft back up, ignoring Archer and my alarmed shouts. The landing was rough too, leaving the flyercraft with a scratch in its white paint on the right side. But we were alive and uninjured, and that was really what mattered.

"In Yellow we are!" I declared, smiling.

Because of the immense height that all central skyscrapers towered at, it didn't take us long to locate Yellow's skyscraper, and we were there in just about half an hour. During this half hour, I noticed myself becoming more relaxed. I felt safer and calmer. The atmosphere here was so much more welcoming than Allight's had been. The people on the streets were kinder. Though it was nowhere near a utopia, and we still witnessed one or two small arguments, it was definitely refreshing after spending time around the Darkened. In fact, I could feel physical effects as well. My fingers, which had been shaking from stress and anxiety from the moment I'd arrived in Allight, were finally still, and smiling seemed somehow easier.

The city was also well-maintained and smelled about a thousand times nicer. There was no graffiti to be found on the walls, and many houses had gardens in front, filled with still unripe fruits and vegetables or colorful flowers.

The strangest thing was that I could *feel* that the city was light. I could feel the difference. I couldn't perfectly describe how, but it was almost like my soul felt closer to home, which was weird. I was actually farther from home that I'd ever been in my life. Traveling on the planet Lucina was uncommon. The cities were situated far apart from one another, and flyer-crafts, which were the fastest form of travel, were restricted to government officials *only* by a strange law. Now that I knew about the Darkened, however, the law made more sense. They were only trying to protect us from the Darkened, lurking in the Midspace. I laughed in my mind, remembering the times when my friends at school and I would make wild theories about why that law existed. Maybe the other cities weren't even real, and only we existed. Up until recently, we couldn't really rule that out.

As we neared the skyscraper, I noticed that it was identical to Green's skyscraper. Same, heavy, wooden door. Same walls, built with the same stone bricks. Even the same dirty "welcome" mat laying at the entrance.

Blue knocked on the door, just like she had on the day it all began, the day of the interview. After a few moments, the door was opened by a girl, maybe a year or two older than us. She was about my height, and wore her long, golden blonde hair in a high ponytail. Her light brown eyes glared at us suspiciously.

Before she could tell us to leave, I announced, "We need to get to your sphorm shelter ASAP! There's no time to explain, but I promise you can trust us. Please, can you let us in?"

"Sorry, what? You really think I'm about to let a bunch of strangers into a government building?" the girl replied.

"Just listen, please. We're on your side. We want what's best for all of Lucina, and to get that, we need to see your sphorm shelter," I pleaded. Though I knew that, for obvious reasons, central skyscrapers, and their sphorm shelters, were off limits to citizens, I continued to hope that maybe we'd convince the girl to let us in. "We work for the leads at Green, and we need help."

"We never received a message that Green was sending anyone," she said skeptically.

Before I could explain our situation, Archer, standing next to me, said, "Look, we are magicals, and *some* of us, by which I mean me, are very power-ful, so I suggest you let us in." He was holding up his right hand, glowing bright red.

"Hey—" I began. I knew that we had the best chance of being let in if we were respectful, but he cut me off before I could tell him.

"Zia, do that light-wall-thing. Show her how the magic likes you."

Light-wall-thing? Oh, he means the touch-activated (or not?) walls. Will it even work on the outside wall? Isn't that only in the shelter, where it's dark? Well, I guess it can't hurt to try, especially if it prevents him from saying something rude. Plus, if it works, I *could be the one to convince this girl to let us in.* I placed my hand on the wall, now more consumed with the thought of being proof that we were magicals than with Archer's disrespectful persuasion tactics. *The magic must really like me… or really feel bad for me*, I thought, as I watched the wall light up. Even in the bright noon light, I could see the mesmerizing glow on the stone bricks.

I knew the girl at the door could see it too, as she turned back inside and called, "Mom, we have some visitors."

I'll admit that it was purely to show off a little more, but I moved my fingertips slowly over the wall, watching the light follow me, and the girl's eyes follow the light in awe.

22

Major Spells

After a moment of awed silence as everyone watched the glowing wall, the elevator door dinged open behind the girl, and a plump woman with a smile on her round face walked towards us. She had the same golden hair as the girl at the door, but her eyes were a light bluish-green. I assumed this was the girl's mother, who she'd called for a few minutes ago.

"What's going on, honey?" She asked the girl.

"These kids say the leads at Green sent them to explore our sphorm shelter," said the girl with a frown.

"Uh," I corrected. "Well, they didn't *send* us, ex-actly." Blue elbowed me in the side, and I quickly added, "But, if they knew why we were here, they'd want us to come inside as well."

"Why are you here, then?" The woman urged us to explain.

"It's a really long story. It would be easier for you to just—" Blue started, but the woman cut her off.

"Then tell me the story," she said. She wasn't rude, but I could tell that there was no way to get out of explaining ourselves at this point, so I didn't bother trying. "We can start with introductions. My name's Joy. I'm the main lead of the city of Yellow. This is my daughter, Saffron." She placed her hands on the shoulders of the girl who'd opened the door. Saffron gave a slight wave.

"My name's Zia. This is my friend, Archer." I pointed to my left. "And this is my other friend, Adella," I pointed to my right, then smirked. "But, you can call her Blue. It's short for—"

"Or, you can use any other, preferably more normal nickname. Like 'Ella,' for instance," Blue suggested, cutting me off.

"But Blue is the most fitting," I argued, still smiling.

She rolled her eyes.

"Well, children, it's nice to meet you. Why don't you get started with the story."

"It all started when—" I stopped abruptly. I wasn't sure if I should mention that Blue was once Darkened. Would it lower our chances of being let in? But, then, what if Joy asked how we even knew about the Pages of Power? How would we explain ourselves? I glanced at Blue, who realized my question and shrugged. "It started years ago, when Blue moved to the city of Green. She ended up in my class, and we made friends…" I told Joy the rest of my story, continuously referring to Adella by the name Blue, and trying not to burst out laughing when she gave me exasperated looks. Blue and Archer filled in their parts of the story, until we'd fully explained why we needed to search the shelter.

As we were telling our story, Joy's face morphed from happy to concerned, and, by the time we were finished, she had asked us if we were okay about a thousand times. "You kids are so brave. You know, you don't have to keep going. You can just stay here. I'll handle the rest. I can call all the cities to—"

I interrupted Joy. I wasn't sure why, but it felt right. Maybe I was being selfish, putting my friends in danger for the sake of an adventure. Maybe I was being heroic, prepared to do anything to save Lucina. Or maybe it was fate. I didn't know, but not for one moment did I regret saying what I said. "Thanks for the offer, but we need to do this ourselves. We'll be fine."

"If you're sure," she relented, still looking as concerned as ever. "You're welcome to explore the shelter. Let me know if you need anything."

"Thank you so much," I smiled, and the three of us entered. We walked to the corner of the room, where I opened the trapdoor the way I'd seen Viola do it back in Green's skyscraper. The stairs leading down the the sphorm shelter looked, like everything else in the building, identical to the stairs in both

Green and in Allight.

In the sphorm shelter, lit, of course, by my hand on the wall, Archer and I followed Blue to where she knew the room would be. Knowing that everything here was identical to the other cities, she unlocked the door with the shard of prism, like we had in Allight. Rushing inside to make up for the time we'd lost explaining our story to Joy, we broke open the glass case and I grabbed the paper inside.

Major Spells

Unlike Minor Spells, Major Spells require a group of people to perform, one of each of the eight magic types: Infrared, Red, Orange, Yellow, Green, Blue, Purple, and Ultraviolet. Major Spells include: Teleportation, Appearance Changes, Time Travel, Light Connection Revival—

I stopped reading. *That should be the right one*, I thought. The rest of the page was just a list of other important spells, which I skimmed over as I searched for directions on how, exactly, I could perform Major Spells. Finding nothing on the front, I flipped the page over. I saw only one sentence on the back:

> To perform a Major Spell, the eight magicals must link hands and focus their energy and imaginations on the spell as a unit.

So, that's it? No rituals? No chants? No potions? Not even a prism? I didn't know exactly what I'd been expecting, but it definitely wasn't to hold hands and think really hard. I showed the back of the paper to Archer and Blue.

"That's it?" Blue asked.

"Apparently," I confirmed.

"Are we sure there isn't another page?" asked Archer.

"Yeah. Who knows? Maybe it really works. The only way to find out is to test it. Plus, we need to find out exactly how many people it can Brighten at once," I said.

"How are we supposed to test it, though? It says we need an Infrared *and* an Ultraviolet, and those are so rare that not even one person with either power has been counted for the past hundred years!" said Blue.

"A hundred years?" I exclaimed. "Do they even exist at all?"

"They did, in the past, if the authors of the Pages chose to write about the Major Spells. What's the point of writing down a spell if the people you need to perform it don't exist?" Archer reasoned.

I tried to be optimistic. "Maybe there are some and the government is just keeping them secret."

"Or, if they exist at all, the government doesn't know they do," said Archer.

"Meaning they're still out there, somewhere," Blue said. "And we could find them!"

"Yeah!" I was glad that I wasn't the only one

looking on the bright side.

"We should work on gathering the team as soon as we can, assuming it's possible at all," Archer announced.

"Let's ask Joy and the other leads here if they have people who can help us and hopefully some secret Infrared and Ultraviolet employees." I started out the door, one hand on the wall and the other gripping the page tightly in determination.

"Hold on. It won't come out," Blue said, and I looked back over my shoulder to see her tugging on the prism shard, which was stuck in the door's keyhole. The string, weakly knotted around the shard, slipped off in her hands, and she looked at me, out of ideas.

"Leave it. I don't need magic protecting me," I declared. I wasn't sure why I was suddenly so confident today, but I didn't mind. I enjoyed being sure of myself, for once.

Blue ignored me, and continued pulling at the prism as hard as she could. Suddenly, the shard snapped in half, leaving most of it in the keyhole, and the other part in Blue's hands. She smiled proudly. "I knew I could do it." She tied the string back onto the prism, then handed it back to me, and we retraced our steps back to the exit.

23

Plan Turned Pointless

Exiting the shelter, we were greeted by Joy, Saffron, and a few security guards. We'd agreed that they would wait outside the shelter while we searched it, and, in the event that we were lying, call in more guards. We knew we weren't lying, but they had no way to tell, so I didn't blame them.

"We found the page!" I announced, smiling as I stepped up onto the floor of the skyscraper.

"What does it say?" asked Joy.

My smile shrank a little. "It says we need eight people to perform the spell. One of each of the eight light colors," I explained.

"Eight?" asked Saffron.

Are Ultraviolet and Infrared really that rare? She really doesn't know about them? That's not a great sign, I thought.

"Infrared and Ultraviolet, too," Blue explained.

Joy looked shocked. "But they're so rare! Are you kids sure?"

"Yup, we're sure." I hesitated. "We were hoping you might know someone who can help us."

My fears came to life as Joy responded. "Sorry, Zia. We don't have any Infrared or Ultraviolet employees here. Maybe you can check the other cities?"

"Oh," I said, disappointed but not surprised. "Maybe we will. Thanks, anyway. We should go now. It's getting late."

"Good luck, children. You'll need it," said Joy. Then, she tried one last time, "Are you completely sure you want to continue with this?"

"We're sure, Joy. You don't need to worry about us. I promise we'll be fine," I reassured her, and we left the skyscraper.

In the flyercraft, on the way back to Allight, we discussed our options. Now that we were aware of just how slim the chance was of us finding people connected to Infrared and Ultraviolet in time, we knew we had to find another way to save Lucina.

Archer, who had read about half of the Minor Spells during the flight to Yellow, said, "Our only real option is to fight them physically." Seeing my face, he added. "Look, I know you don't want to. *I* don't want to. But we *have* to. There's no other choice."

"But—"

"Do you want to save Lucina or not?"

"Yes," I said, finally giving in. "I'd really been hopeful that we could Brighten them, though."

"I know, but I also know that there's no other option. Fighting would be easier, too, since most of the Minor Spells are perfect for battle," Archer insisted.

I couldn't think of anything else to say, so I just nodded. For the rest of the flight, I was lost in thought, and Blue was focused on not letting the fly-ercraft crash, leaving Archer with no one to talk to, so we sat in silence.

Maybe I'm not meant to be a hero, after all, I thought for the millionth time since I'd found myself in Allight. *I tried, and I failed. The chance is too slim. We'll never find an Ultraviolet* and *an Infrared in time. There is* no way *to perform a Light Connection Revival spell. There is no way to peacefully take back Allight. I'm an idiot. A powerless idiot. I wasted our time. We could've been preparing, but no. I just* had *to drag Blue and Archer all the way to Yellow. What's wrong with me? Why couldn't I have just thought log-ically?* I fidgeted with the shard of prism around my neck, even more broken than before. *That's my fault, too.* I *was the one who suggested we use it as a lock pick.*

Not only was I worried about my worthiness of the role of hero, I was also nervous about the battle ahead. I knew that I'd have to watch people fighting, and possibly killing. Maybe even do it myself. I wasn't ready. As much as Lucina would benefit from the clearing of the Darkened from Allight, the thought of having to hurt people made me feel sick. Plus, I didn't know anything about fighting. What if I was the reason we failed? What if I did something stupid and ruined our chances of saving the planet? I had no way of knowing it *wouldn't* happen. Yeah, I definitely was *not* the right one for this job.

I suddenly remembered the night before, when Blue had reassured me that I had the power to do anything. According to her, I was the one who'd brought her back to the good side. *I don't care what Blue says*, I thought angrily. *She was just trying to be nice. What does she know? I've probably* already *ruined everything by insisting we fly to Yellow. I was never meant to be a hero. In fact, right now, I should tell her to fly to Green instead, to take me back to where I belong. I'll resign from my job, which I didn't really earn at all, and I'll go back to my old life. I may have been a nobody, but everyone was safer back then.*

"Blue," I said, wiping the tears I hadn't realized

I'd cried off of my face.

She turned to face me. "Yeah?"

I hesitated. Something inside wouldn't let me quit. Not like this. I just couldn't. I had to finish what I'd started. Quitting somehow seemed scarier than the battle I knew I would have to fight. Maybe, deep down inside, I still believed in myself. "Never mind," I said, turning my head to look out the flyercraft's window again.

24

Almost Killed! ALMOST!

In the skyscraper back at Allight, the three of us, thrilled to see the communicator had finished refreshing and mostly worked again (it could still only send messages to one city at a time) sent a message for backup to Green, then waited out the 5 hours it took for the flyercrafts to arrive anxiously at Archer's house. I practiced physical fighting, how to dodge attacks and how to punch properly, while Blue and Archer, who had actual powers, practiced the Minor Spells that were listed in Allight's Pages. A few times, envious thoughts went through my head, as I wished I could have magic like my friends. I ignored these thoughts, and continued practicing. I couldn't let what

I wanted distract me from what I needed to do.

By the time help from Green arrived it was almost midnight, but the three of us were nowhere near tired. I was buzzing with nervous energy. Would we win? Would we lose? Would we make it out alive? *Hopefully this works*, I thought, watching the first flyercraft land just outside the city, the green stripe on its tail barely visible in the dark. The other nine flyercrafts landed near it.

The message we'd sent had contained all the details about what was to occur, so the three of us only had to wait for help to arrive, then run and join them. We did exactly that, and, in a matter of half an hour, we were ready to attack. *That was fast*, I thought to myself. I knew that the danger was near now. However, I also knew that, though we were a small force, we had two huge advantages over the Darkened: magic and surprise. I couldn't deny that, even through the anxiety, I felt a hope deep inside that we *could* do this.

Before I knew it, the battle had begun. Let me tell

you this, I did not feel one bit heroic. In fact, I felt quite the opposite. I felt small and scared, lost and dazed. Everyone around me seemed to know exactly what to do, but I had no idea where to start. My surroundings were pure chaos. People were everywhere, and so were screams and bright blasts of color.

Blue was trying to organize the chaos around us and cheer our side up, while Archer was leading a group towards the skyscraper, to take it back. I didn't really do much. I just stood there, taking in my surroundings. I wasn't sure what to do. I could barely hear myself think over the chaos, and all I wanted was for things to have gone another way, for us to have been able to find a way to Brighten the Darkened. For the people of the past to have discovered another way to perform Major Spells. For Light Connection Revival to be a Minor Spell instead, able to be performed by just one person. But, no. The battle had already begun, and there was no going back now.

Once, I felt a brush against my arm, and turned to see an enemy with a knife next to me. Without thinking, I ran as far away as I could, blinded by an instinct to get away from the danger. It backfired when I realized I'd run straight into a group of more enemies. What had I done?

Panicked, I said, "You don't have to hurt me! I'm powerless! What am I going to do other than just stand here? I can't hurt you, I swear." Looking back, it was probably a horrible idea to let the enemy know just how helpless I was, but it had been done already, and it was not like they believed me anyway.

"Liar," hissed one tall woman. "Look at her. She has a piece of prism around her neck. She's some kind of prism guardian or something."

"Please, I'm no prism guardian. I'm a nobody," I insisted, but the Darkened, being evil and all, clearly didn't care to listen.

"You think you're so clever," said the same woman. "Trying to trick me, but it's not going to work." She slashed her sword at my face, and my arm swung up in from of my face by reflex. My eyes shut as tight as possible, as if maybe the blade would disappear if I couldn't see it. A moment passed, and I realized I'd felt a swipe, but not much else. *Good to know*, I thought, no less scared than the moment I'd seen the sword. *Getting hit by a sword doesn't hurt. So I guess that's how the heroes do it.*

"WHAT?" Came an enraged voice.

I slowly opened my eyes and studied my forearm. Perfectly unharmed. Had she missed? But I'd felt the swipe. "Unbelievable," I breathed. I didn't have time to think before the man next to the evil woman started shouting.

"It's her prism! The prisms must hold magic!"

"Get the prism!" the woman shouted.

I took off the necklace—probably a bad move, now that I thought back on it—and stared at it. "Thank you," I whispered, but the shard lay motionless in my palm.

The next thing I knew, I was surrounded by people. Everyone wanted the prism. My hand closed on the sharp shard, gripping it with all my strength. I wouldn't let the Darkened get to it. I tried to send it a message. I didn't know if it would even work. I wasn't looking at it. It wasn't even a whole prism anymore, but I didn't care. It was my only hope. *Clear the crowd*, I shouted in my mind. *Help me! Wait, maybe in pictures?* I tried to visualize the crowd clearing off of me, going back to whoever they were fighting before. No, that wasn't a good idea. I didn't want others to get hurt either. Maybe… could it work? There was only one way to find out. *While you're at it*, I added. *Brighten them all. Do it.*

All of a sudden, my vision filled with a bright, white flash.

25

The Brightening

Though all I could see was white, I felt my feet slowly lifted off of the ground until I was levitating. My eyes may have been seeing white, but in my mind, I could see *everything*. Just like how I'd seen a flash of white when I'd cleared the sphorm, but also seen the land flashing below me. Time froze now, and a wave of light rushed over the city, starting from where I was. People went from looking angry, sad, hurt, scared to neutral faces with closed eyes. The dark clouds in the sky cleared.

I saw well beyond Allight. I saw the entire planet now. The wave of light was rushing over everything else as well, Brightening the Darkened in Red, in

Leila Sahabi

Purple, in the Midspace, and spying in the other cities.

I breathed in, then out. I realized that the prism had worked… or had it? I suddenly remembered the day of the interview, the day that this adventure had started. When Cyrus had shown Blue the prism, hadn't he said that it focused the light magic *inside* of someone? But wouldn't that mean that the prism had no magic of its own? That it just reflected one's inner magic? And that would mean that… Could it really be true? I knew deep down that it was.

I was in a world of my own. I *did* have magic, after all. Somehow, my soul knew. All this time that I'd been wishing for magic, it had been inside of me. But I was seeing *white*, and the wave of light rushing over Lucina was white as well. White light, as I'd learned in school, was not really white, but a mix of all the colors in the spectrum. I now knew I wasn't powerless, but nor was I just one color of magic. I was all of them. I was all light. I was allight.

I was Zia Allight.

The white slowly faded back into the darkness of the night as my feet sank to the ground. In my hand, the shard of prism had shattered completely, but none of the tiny pieces of glass had cut me. *Am I... invincible? That sword too, the way it didn't cut me, and the way I wasn't hurt when I cleared the sphorm back in Green...* My theory was disproved, however, when a piece of glass scratched me as I brushed the dust off of my palm. *Maybe only sometimes*, I concluded, trying to stay hopeful.

Then, I realized that everyone, all the Darkened, and all the people from Green, were staring at me, wide-eyed, in complete, awed silence.

"Uh, hello." I gave a little wave, unsure of what to say.

Shouts of, "How did you do that?" and, "What *are* you?" and similar things erupted from everywhere in the crowd. I heard familiar voices, and unfamiliar ones alike. I watched the leads of Green, all but Grandma Mari, who was clearly too old to fight, pushing their way through the crowd to get to me.

"How did you do that?" Emery asked.

"I don't really know," I said. "But the prism is completely shattered." I pointed down at the dust that was once the prism of the city of Green.

"We don't care about that. They're replaceable," said Rose. "Are *you* okay?"

"Yeah, I'm fine." I was tired, but I realized that, under the exhaustion, I was feeling more alive than ever. I was proud of what I'd done, and excited, now knowing what I could really do. "You know how white light is a mix of all the colors on the spectrum? I think I am, too. Allight, you know?"

"She's right," Sapphire agreed, a look of realization visible in her deep blue eyes. "Her test results didn't mean powerless... they meant all-powerful!"

"Isn't it funny how my last name's Allight, too? The city of All Light. I'd just always assumed that my ancestors lived at Allight, but... could there have been others like me?"

"Maybe," Sapphire said. "But, I would think that if there were, we'd know. Someone would've written it down. There would be rumors, stories, myths. Plus, I know for a fact that the magic loves tales of fate and destiny. It is much more likely that you were born to do great things, Zia."

I was born to do great things! I could barely believe what I was hearing! All of that self-doubt had turned out to be false!

Just then, I noticed Blue and Archer running towards me.

"Was that *you*?" Blue asked, awed. "How did you do that? What even was that?"

Before I could respond, Archer said, "So, you got what you wanted in the end, huh? You found a way to Brighten the city."

"Yeah, I did, and I don't even know how I did it. Apparently, my test results didn't mean powerless after all. They meant all-powerful. I do have magic, but not just one color. All of them!"

"I told you so! I called it!" Blue declared proudly. "I knew you could do it!"

"And Sapphire thinks I was born to do great

things!" I realized how far I'd come. Just a few days ago, the leads had been accusing me of being a spy for the Darkened, of breaking the prism (which, to be fair, I had done, but not in the way that they had thought). Now, they were telling me that I was destined to be a hero.

I realized, finally, that I was right. I was right to have kept persisting for a job at the skyscraper. I was right to have tried to clear the sphorm. I was right to have kept insisting we try to find a way to take back Allight that didn't involve injuring others. I was right to have told Joy that we didn't need help and that we would be fine. I was the right one for the role, and now I knew it. Everyone knew it. So, I really *was* meant to be a hero in the end.

26

The Magic

As tired as we realized we were, now that the anxiety about the battle ahead had faded, Archer, Blue, and I had unanimously agreed that we should fly back to Green. Blue and I were completely ready to be back home, and Archer would be safer the farther he could get from his Corrupt parents. Of course, having no license and very limited experience, Blue wasn't allowed to be the pilot, and an adult had to come with us. I didn't care. I was asleep the entire time.

I was floating again. I could feel it. It was still as

strange as ever, but I felt safe. In this glowing place, nothing could bother me. Nothing but the figure.

In the distance, I could see—sense, actually; like everything else, the figure was glowing. I couldn't really *see* anything—a figure. A humanoid figure, but I could tell it wasn't a human. And it was approaching. It wasn't walking, more floating. *Do I look like that, too?* I wondered.

As it neared, I noticed that it had no features. Not even a solid shape. It was constantly moving and flowing in such a familiar way. I realized that it looked exactly like the glowing sign on Emery's office door, and like the glowing bricks of the skyscrapers. It had no eyes, but I knew it could sense me. Like so many times during that day, I didn't really know how I knew.

It had no mouth, but it spoke. "I see you're now cognizant of your true potential." Her words, echoey but solid, quiet but powerful, seemed to come from everywhere at once, not just out of the figure herself.

The only thing I could think to say was, "Uh…

Lucinian please?"

And the figure… burst out laughing? "You think I really speak like that?"

"Uh," I was confused. Who was this figure? Suddenly, a thought popped into my head. *She's the magic.* Immediately afterwards, I thought, *How do I know that?* I realized that I knew it the same way I'd known not to ask Blue to change courses and fly back home to Green, the same way I'd known that I did, in fact, have magic.

"I'm just being formal," the figure laughed. "Now, you're a smart girl. I know you know who I am, but it's protocol to go over this. I'm the Magic— well, your idea of what it is, anyway." She looked down at herself. "I seem to be humanoid this time, but that's unimportant. We have some urgent things to discuss."

"So, the Magic is a conscious being?" I asked.

"Oh, yeah."

"How long has it—have you—been a living thing?"

"Not living. Conscious. They're different. I've existed since the very beginning of the universe," she corrected me.

"Whoa. What do you do all day? Where do you live? Is there anyone else there with you?"

"We're getting off topic here. Yes, there are others. You can't expect *one* spirit to run *everything*, can you? But that's unimportant right now."

"Fair point," I said reluctantly. "But at least tell me this. Am I the only one?"

"Well, you're not the only one with magic that doesn't involve one specific color of light, but you *are* the universe's sole Allight. The only one ever to exist. See what I did, there, with your last name, and all? I've been planning this for generations, you know." She smiled triumphantly, clearly proud of how she'd made things play out.

"Is it true that I'm destined to do great things? What *are* those great things?" I asked eagerly.

"That is true, and that's what I'm here to talk to you about. You see this?"

A picture of a planet appeared in my mind, like the way the wave of light engulfing Lucina had appeared before. But this planet wasn't Lucina. This planet had more than one landmass. "Yeah. Where is that?"

"That's Earth. The ancestors of everyone living on Lucina came from this planet."

I knew that. All students on Lucina briefly learn about Earth, but contact with them was cut thousands of years ago for reasons known only to the government, and I'd never bothered to ask. Nobody really knew much about them, and not many people cared. "I know."

"And they need help." Pictures flashed in my mind of people killing each other over land, over clothing, over a belief that some were better than others. They used weird machines that made loud noises. I'd never seen them before. I saw people yelling at each other, people stealing, people calling names, people crying, people protesting, people being arrested, people dying. The plants were burning, the air was gray, the oceans were filled with trash. It looked just like Allight yesterday. And it hit me that it *was* like Allight. The entire planet. It was Darkened.

"It's all evil," I said, stunned. How could a whole planet be so... awful? How could people live there? How did it get like that? *When* did it get like that?

"Most of it, yes, but not all of it." I saw more pictures, but this time they were of people helping each other, helping the environment, helping other creatures. But, even with the proof that not everything on this planet was terrible, I got a sense that the bad outweighed the good most of the time.

"Still. That's a lot of Darkness," I said.

"I know. But you have the power to change that. You are very special. You hold the strongest power in all the universe. Trust me. I would know. I gave it to you. And I know that I can rely on you to be responsible with this power. You will use it for the greater good of the universe, and not for personal gain. From this moment on, you, Zia Allight, are in charge of the Brightening of the universe," the figure announced.

I couldn't tell if her voice was echoing in the room or in my mind. It was all such a big task. Such an exciting task. I was going to Brighten the whole universe! It sounded so overwhelmingly amazing. "Does that mean there are more planets like Earth?" I asked.

"It's a huge universe. What do you think?"

"Yes. And I have to try to Brighten them all. No. I'm *going to* Brighten them all."

"That's the spirit! Wow, I wish some of the beings I work with had *that* attitude towards tasks this big."

"And if there are other planets, are there other types of magic?" I was eager to learn everything I could about the universe I was to fix.

"Hmm. I don't know. Are there?" She knew. She definitely knew. How could she not? She was the Magic itself. "*That* is for you to discover."

"Well, I'm excited. This has been my dream for *so* long!"

"Just so you know, this was always my plan. Never forget that your dreams are there to guide you."

"If only you'd tell the leads," I groaned.

"They had a right to be suspicious, and you know it," said the Magic. "But you reminded me. Back on Lucina, no one's going to believe that you talked to me. They'll think it was just some weird dream sparked by the events of last night. You need to take back proof. Give me those pages."

"Pa—" I started, then I realized that the Pages of Power that we'd found so far, the ones from Allight, Yellow, and Green, were in my right hand. I handed them to her. A flash of light surrounded the Pages and when it faded, a book was left in the "hands" of the figure. She handed it back to me.

"There we go. Now it's restored," she said.

The book, heavy and thick, had a brown leather cover, and printed on it in big, golden letters were the words "The Pages of Power." Flipping through, I realized that the page from Green was no longer wrinkled. The Pages really had been restored.

"You show this to the leads. Tell them that I gave it to you. Tell them everything I told you. Oh, except that stuff about my coworkers! Don't tell them that."

I nodded obediently.

"And, when you find the rest of the Pages, which I'm sure won't take too long, I will see you again to complete the book."

I nodded again, glad that I'd be seeing the Magic again. Since my power was so unique, I knew that there was no way the leads and I could figure it out ourselves. We would need guidance from the Magic.

"Well, now that I've dumped a giant load of work on you, it looks like it's time for you to go. I'll see you later. I promise," she said, as the brilliant glow began to fade away.

"Go where?" I asked.

"Wake up."

"What?"

27

Reunion

"Oh, how the tables have turned! Wake up," said Blue.

"We're home?" I mumbled sleepily.

"Yeah, and your parents are here... and they're yelling."

"Why?" I asked. As I fully woke up, I noticed a book in my hand. That hadn't been there when we had gotten into the flyercraft. *Where did I—oh, the Magic. She gave it to me.* I also noticed that the suns hadn't risen yet, which meant that it was way too early to wake up.

"You being in danger. Get up and tell them you're fine."

"Oh, ok," I said, trying to fall back asleep.

"I'm enjoying this so much! Revenge feels great!" said Blue.

Suddenly remembering the moment I'd woken her up, I realized I wasn't going to let her win. I stood up, and walked toward the flyercraft door, the Pages of Power in my hand.

"How is this legal?" my mom was shouting at the leads.

"You put her in danger without consulting us," my dad added.

"Sir, Ma'am, I believe there has been a misunderstanding. We tried our best to stop her, but your daughter *chose* to use the prism," Emery was explaining calmly.

Both my parents looked ready to throw hands. Rage and worry were all over their faces, and the dark circles under their eyes told me that they hadn't slept since the day I'd cleared the sphorm. I started slowly towards them, then I ran into their open arms. "Mom, Dad, I missed you so much." Tears filled my eyes.

"Zia!" my dad exclaimed. "We won't let them put you in any more danger. Don't worry."

"We love you so much," said my mom.

"Wait," I said, pulling away from my parents. "*They* didn't put me in danger. He's telling the truth. *I* did. *I* chose this all. Don't get mad at the leads."

"But—" my dad started.

I continued, "*I* took the prism and blasted away the sphorm. Those clouds you saw on the day before it all started? Those would've killed us all. Luckily, all they ruined was my hair. *I* found the Pages of Power." I held up the book. "*I* Brightened all of the Sad Darkened. Those are the ones that can be re-Brightened. And, most importantly, *I* talked to the Magic. The spirit that gives us all our personalities, our hopes and dreams. She restored the Pages and she told me that I really am destined for great things. She told me that I have the strongest power in the universe."

"But that's not safe! You're too young to be a hero," my mom was saying, shaking her head. "Why don't you just leave it to the qualified adults?"

"I'm very qualified. The Magic herself told me that I'm the key to the Brightening of the universe!" I insisted. "She showed me the planet we all came from. Earth. It needs help. Almost everyone there is Darkened. But *I* can change that, if you give me permission."

Then, I remembered the way I was uninjured after the sphorm, the way the sword didn't hurt me, the way the bits of shattered prism didn't cut me while I had been floating. Now that I thought about it, I could recognize a pattern. Maybe I was invulnerable while I was using my magic. Maybe that would convince my parents. "Listen, I think I'm invulnerable while I'm using the magic. I'm ninety-nine percent sure. *Now* will you let me save the universe?"

My parents exchanged a glance. "If you really are the only one…" my dad began.

"And if you're sure it's safe…" my mom continued.

"And if you really want to," said my dad.

"You can go," my mom finished.

"Yes!" I exclaimed.

28

Future

"There isn't any way that working for the government can get me out of having to go to school, is there?" I asked hopefully.

"Absolutely not," said Emery.

I was discussing my future as the most powerful person in the universe with the leads. I may have been all-powerful, but they were still the adults, so they were in charge of me. Outside, Blue and Archer were waiting to hear the plans.

"But what if I have to save a planet in the middle of math class?"

"She makes a good point," Viola said.

"We'll think about that when it actually happens,"

said Rose.

"Fine," I said. "So, how is this going to work? And what about my friends? What happens with them?"

"For you, work will start at twelve o'clock P.M. every weekday—"

I interrupted her, "Hold on. If you six can make work start at *twelve*, why did the interview have to be so early?" Though I would've gone even if it had meant pulling an all-nighter, waking up so early had been more than inconvenient. My parents, both early risers, had been confused as to why I was up so early and where in the world I was going.

"Oh, that was a test. We had to see just how determined our candidates were. That's a key part of being a hero, but you know that already. When the school year starts, the time moves to four. You will be trained to use your power to the best of your ability, and will also help us put together and study the Pages of Power," Rose explained. "As for your friends, we'll be happy to test Archer's abilities and, if he qualifies for a position, offer him one. Since his parents turned out to be Corrupt Darkened, and therefore not Brightenable, we can also provide him a housing unit in the skyscraper, all-expenses-paid. Adella is both a traitor, and not powerful enough to join. She's at seventy four point three percent, and our minimum for entry is seventy five. Howe—"

A sudden burst of anger flared up inside me. "She's not even one percent off. You can make an exception, can't you?"

"I know it seems unfair, but we have to follow our own rules, Zia."

"I, as the most powerful person in the universe, order you to let her join."

Rose shook her head. "That's not how it works. You're still a minor, and I'm an adult, and you'll soon learn that one of the most important parts of having a lot of power is putting restrictions on yourself. But, you didn't let me finish. Considering Adella *did* play a part in saving the planet, she will not be put in jail."

That was it? Not being put in jail? I wanted to

scream. It wasn't fair. I had gotten so far. Everything had been fixable up until this point. As a last resort, I blurted out, "She knows the secrets of the Pages of Power already."

"Oh. That's a fair point. We still can't let her join as an employee, but she can be one of our colleagues. She can work *with* us, but not *for* us, and she's welcome in the skyscraper as needed."

"Thank you!" I said. It wasn't exactly perfect, but it was a solution, and it meant that Blue would still work with me, so it was better than nothing.

"You're welcome. She's been here for a while, so I assume she has a place to stay already?"

"Yeah. She'll stay with her parents. They were Brightened by my light wave." I knew that it would take a while for Adella and her parents to mend their relationship. Since childhood, Adella had been less of a child to her parents, and more of a tool. She'd explained to Archer and I that the reason she'd disappeared as a child was because of her parents. They'd discovered her magic and kept her locked in their house like a prisoner. For weeks, she had been deprived of positive human interaction, until, finally, she gave in to the Darkness. But now, all three of them were back on the bright side, and I was confident that they would make up.

I stood up to leave, but Rose said, "Oh, and one more thing. Tell your friend, Adella, that she's free to keep the flyercraft she stole. It's heavily damaged and not worth repairing."

"A whole flyercraft? I will. Thank you," I said smiling, as I exited the meeting room.

"Well?" asked Blue. "Can we stay?"

"Yeah! They told me that you can work with the government, but not for them." I smiled mischievously. "Who's the one allowed the job now? And, as for Archer," I turned toward him. "They're going to test you. If you qualify, which you probably do, you get a job. And, Blue, you get to keep the flyercraft you stole!"

"But how?" Archer asked. "I'm three years too young to legally buy a house, and my parents…"

"Oh, they're giving you a free room. The whole skyscraper's supervised by the government, so you don't have to be sixteen," I explained.

He smiled. "Nice."

"Wait a minute. Did you say I get to *keep* the flyercraft?" asked Blue.

"Yeah," I said. "Rose said it's too dama—"

"Yes! Yes! Yes! Yes! Yes!"

29

Sunrise

From the East Balcony, the place where I'd blast-ed away the sphorm, I stood by myself, watching the two suns appear over the horizon. It was probably the first time in years I'd woken up to see a sunrise, not counting the dawn as I walked towards Allight. On that day, I'd only *seen* the sunrise, not really watched it or enjoyed it. I had been too consumed with won-dering where on Lucina I was.

I thought about how sunrises looked a lot like sunsets. The sky turned orange. The clouds turned pink. People loved watching both events.

It's kind of funny, I thought, *the way sunrises feel like sunsets and beginnings feel like ends.* The day had felt like a conclusion to my adventure, but, in reality, my story was just starting.

The leads and I had explained everything to my parents: the magic, the sphorms, the Darkened, and everything that had happened during the past few days. They'd signed a contract that said they wouldn't disclose anything that they'd learned, and they'd told me just how proud they were that I was making changes in the world and following my dreams.

I wasn't sure how to feel.

Excited?

Nervous?

Happy?

Scared?

What did the future hold for me, and was I ready for it? What kind of things would I do? What secrets would I uncover? Where would I go? Who would I meet? How long would it take to Brighten the entire universe? *What* would it take?

The one thing I didn't doubt, however, was that I was enough. The leads trusted me, and the magic herself had told me that I was meant for this, but, most importantly, I believed in myself. I knew that, whatever, it took, I'd be willing to do it. And I'd be completely able. No more self-doubt. I'd gotten this far and I was capable of going much, much farther.

I was the only Allight (that was what we'd named my power. After me! Can you believe it?) in the history of the universe! I was destined to Brighten people, even planets. I was proud of who I was, what I'd done, and what I would continue to do during my life. I could do things that would require eight people to do normally.

Eight people, including an Ultraviolet and an Infrared, which reminded me. The leads and I had agreed that, as we began our efforts to Brighten the Dark parts of the universe, we'd search through it for anyone connected to Infrared or Ultraviolet. By having at least one full team that could replace me if needed, we would make the universe-Brightening process go by faster.

It was all so new and exciting to me. My lifelong

dreams were finally coming true. All of them. I was a hero. I was special. I knew it didn't end here. I had a whole universe to explore and save. A Darkened planet to rescue, more possible types of magic to discover, Ultraviolet and Infrared magicals to find, new friends and enemies to make, and I would be doing this all with the best friend group I could ever ask for. Adventure was ahead and I couldn't be happier.

I watched the sunrise for a few minutes longer, taking deep breaths and appreciating the peace. I hadn't been fully relaxed for days, and, though I was excited for the adventures ahead, I wouldn't mind a break. Plus, I had figured out that creating blasts of magic, as I'd done twice in the past few days, was very exhausting. I knew that, the minute I reached my house, I'd fall asleep.

From high above the city of Green, I watched as the orange sky began fading to blue, the clouds turned from white to pink, and the city began to wake up. The streets became more and more crowded as people left their houses to walk to work. I smiled at the suns and turned to go inside.

As unfamiliar as the situation was, as inexperienced as I was, it felt right. Like I was meant for this. Like I'd found my place in the world.

It felt like home.

THE END

Made in the USA
Middletown, DE
13 January 2024

47551506R00109